Lock Down Publications and Ca$h Presents

WHITE BOYS 2

Black Ice

Written By

BANDEMIC

First Edition 2026

Printed in the United States of America

Lock Down Publications
P.O. Box 944
Stockbridge, GA 30281
www.lockdownpublications.com

Like our page on Facebook: Lock Down Publications
www.facebook.com/lockdownpublications.ldp

Stay Connected with Us!

Text **LOCKDOWN** to 22828 to stay up-to-date with new releases, sneak peaks, contests and more…

Like our page on Facebook:
Lock Down Publications

Join Lock Down Publications/The New Era Reading Group

Visit our website:
www.lockdownpublications.com

Follow us on Instagram:
Lock Down Publications

Email Us: We want to hear from you!

Chapter 1

Teddy Lee was sitting on the hood of his Pontiac GTO with a joint of Sour Diesel balanced between his lips. *Westland Drank* was the go-to establishment in Lee County—a bikers' joint that catered to every inglorious bastard underneath the southwest flag. As the faint orange glow of the evening sunset stretched across their backs, the sizable parking lot of *Westland Drank* was filling to capacity with a mix of Chevelles, Thunderbirds, Novas, choppers, and pickup trucks in all shapes and sizes.

Teddy Lee watched Brandlyn and Thelma—two meth whores from Bluff City, Tennessee, dance loosely to a popular Garth Brooks song blasting from his Pontiac. He had no real interest in the two redheads and just simply saw them as a much-needed distraction from the storm brewing in his head. Bobbi and Merle's treacherous betrayal still held firm to his emotions, clouding his sense of self more and more as the months progressed. There were nights when he nearly threw himself behind the steering wheel of his GTO and gunned it to Norton, ready to strangle the life out of Merle—his soul burning for retribution.

After taking a chug of his beer, Teddy Lee's brother, Cliff, hollered the hoorah of a cowboy, then said. "Hot damn, son. Who the hell invented leggings, huh?" Another hoorah followed while eyeing the meth whores hungrily, then: "Whoever it is, we need a holiday in their honor, I tell ya."

"With a parade," added Grant, the youngest brother.

Teddy Lee laughed. The weed had taken effect, but his brother's accreditation of the matching white leggings that hugged their jiggly soft asses marvelously, was head-on.

Minutes later, a small red Toyota pulled up, and Teddy Lee knew it to be Jainy Reynold's car—Bobbi's best friend. Teddy Lee and his brothers were all staring at their reflections in the tinted mirror, then the driver's side window slowly rolled down. Bobbi sat in the passenger seat, staring directly ahead as if she was in a trance. Teddy Lee could tell she'd been crying, but he' d been through his own share of tears, so he wasn' t about to waste time caring about hers. A group of motorcycles rumbled past and Teddy Lee pretended to be interested in the riders.

Cliff and Grant both glared at Bobbi displeasingly. They knew the details of her deceit, and in their opinion, she wasn't welcome there.

Jainy got out of the car and addressed Teddy Lee. "She wants to talk to you," she said,

"Stop being mean, Cliff. This is nobody's business, but theirs," she added.

"Then why the hell are you here?" Grant shot back.

"She—"

Teddy Lee cut her off. "What's there to talk about? There's no taking back what she did."

Jainy sighed, because she knew that her friend had messed up bad, but her mother always told her, "Where there's a will, there's a way, sugar." And Jainy truly believed in that terminology.

"Wouldn't hurt any to hear her out," she told him.

"Like hell it wouldn't. She's a bottom feeder," Cliff exclaimed. "Merle ain't nothing but a two bit-"

"Get us some beers, Jainy," Teddy Lee said, hopping down from the hood of his car.

Jainy nodded tightly and headed for the door of the bar.

"I'll be back," Teddy Lee told his brothers.

"Man, don't do it, Teddy," Grant said.

"I said I'll be back," he responded tartly, and Grant backed down.

Teddy Lee climbed into the driver's seat of the Toyota, and Bobbi smiled at him.

"Hey," she said,

Teddy Lee ignored her and simply put the car into drive and pulled off. Turning left onto the main road, he headed past the Crawford plantation, shrouded in a dense cloud of dust as rustlers drove a herd of wild horses toward Devil's Valley.

"Why are you here?" Teddy Lee asked her.

"We need to talk."

He looked at her, both of their eyes heavy with sadness. "About?"

"Us."

"There is no us, Bobbi. You—"

She cut him off. "I'm pregnant."

Teddy Lee's jaw clenched. This angered him even more. "Who's the father?"

Bobbi blinked, insulted. "Teddy, oh my god. Really? You are."

He grumbled. "Yeah, I doubt that, you bitch."

Bobbi looked down at her hands. "I'm almost certain that it's yours, Teddy."

Teddy Lee floored the gas pedal. "Almost ain't good enough," he shouted.

Bobbi's head shot up as the car hurtled off the edge of a steep ravine.

"Teddy!" she cried, falling against the dashboard as the Toyota flipped, and flipped and flipped, tumbling through the air before nose-diving into a seven-foot boulder, and catching fire.

Poooghh!

Black smoke raced to the heavens, and a few cowboys from the Crawford plantation kicked their mares into gear and galloped across the street to the ravine . . .

. . . Teddy Lee pushed the thought of that tragic day out of his mind and took a pull from his cigarette. Memories of Bobbi always brought a tear to his eye. She was the only woman he'd ever loved, and that kind of love never came easy. He had hoped to kill him and Bobbi that day and end his miserable state of mind, but somehow, he reckoned that God had a purpose for him and Bobbi, because they both survived that crash by the grace of His power, though he wasn't sure why.

Brushing his hand across the nape of his neck, Teddy Lee caressed one of the many scars that he received from that accident. He wondered if Bobbi's scars ever made her think about him and the good times they'd once shared.

Teddy Lee sat on the front porch of one of his many meth labs in his beloved Lee County, waiting on the recipe so he may apply it to his latest batch and finally stop making those damn trips to Asheville.

His phone rang. It was Cunningham calling.

"Yeah," he answered.

"Boss, the boy ain't talking."

Teddy Lee sighed. He was tired of toying around with these sons of a bitches. First, Dog Man and his incompetent son, Jaxon, botched the hit on Savannah. Then they couldn't pinpoint Errol's location to off him, which would've definitely broke Merle down and made him give them what they wanted. So they formulated a hair-brained attempt to fake Jaxon's death in hopes of getting to Merle—Failure! Failure! Failure! Failure!

Enough

Teddy Lee reached onto a table for a machete, his voice low and cold. "Bring that chicken-shit summabitch to me. I'll cut it out 'em."

Chapter 2

Errol and Harley rushed through the doors of the hospital and up to the front desk. Errol's heart was pounding against his rib cage, and beads of sweat rode the edge of his hairline.

He spoke to the nurse seated at the computer, and she informed him that his family was around the corner in the waiting room, just left of the ATM machine. Errol grabbed Harley by the hand and ran for the corridor.

During the time that Errol and Harley were feeding the homeless in Tent City, Errol remembered that his phone was set to 'Do Not Disturb'. As soon as he disabled the setting, he received a call from his mother, whereupon he learned that not only were his parents worried sick about him, but also that tragedy had struck again. First, Dog Man was murdered. Now, Savannah and Davie were fighting for their lives, and Squirrel was locked away in a cell for multiple homicides.

There were several family members present in the waiting room. They were all drenched in worry—arms crossed over their chests, pacing the floor. A man pounded on the plexiglass of a vending machine, an infant wailed in the arms of its mother, and children ran amok, disrupting doctors who were attempting to speak quietly with relatives of their patients.

Errol spotted his parents talking to Sheriff Dougherty in a far corner of the room. They didn't notice his presence.

"Hey, Errol," Cousin Bella said, embracing him.

Others followed suit, spiking a cluster of resentment in Harley. This was what she had always wanted from her own family—love. She glanced at the tattoo on Bella's forearm—a marking that every member of their family of age had, Errol included—and she wanted that tattoo so bad she could taste it.

Errol and Harley closed in on his parents but were careful not to interrupt their exchange with the sheriff, picking up bits and pieces like nosy little eavesdroppers.

"Do y'all have any idea why this may have happened?" Dougherty asked.

"No," answered Merle.

"What about Chicken Hawk?"

"What about him?" Freah spoke.

"Well, we know that he's been operating out of that apartment for quite some time, and although he wasn't present when we arrived, I know that he's hands-on with the daily ins and outs of drug transactions in that building. Maybe, y'know, there was a falling out between your brother and ol' Chicken Hawk?"

"I know nothing of the kind, friend," Merle expressed. "But I seriously doubt it. Not our style to mingle with or against crack dealers."

Dougherty gave him a knowing smirk. "Reckon we all know that he sold other drugs besides crack, Merle."

Merle shrugged. "Hey. I'll lie for you before I lie to you, James. You know that."

Dougherty took a deep breath. Merle was a lot of things, but he'd never been a bullshitter. Dougherty looked deep into his eyes, searching for a possible answer to all of this, and all he saw was sincerity. Maybe Merle and Freah were truly in the dark about the shooting in Inkly Bottom, but how far into the dark was the question? They were the biggest meth dealers in the region, so how much really went undetected in their lives?

"Okay. Well, I won't bother you folks any longer," Dougherty said. "Prayers to the family."

"Thank you."

"Mom. Dad." Errol spoke

Freah and Merle whirled around and a yip escaped Freah's mouth before she wrapped her arms around her son's neck.

"Errol!" she shrieked.

Merle joined the bunch, pulling them both into his arms. Harley's eyes watered, but she fought back her tears.

Freah cried her eyes out. Harley had never seen her mother express such emotion over her or Holly. Harley looked at the screen of her phone. It was nearly midnight and neither one of her parents had called in concern for her whereabouts. Hurtful, to say the least.

"I'm okay, I'm all right." Errol said, reassuring his parents that he was fine.

Freah released him and saw his busted lip and bruised face. "What hap—" then locked eyes with Harley. Anger sped through her features. "What the hell is she doing here?"

This raised alarm and caused Harley to take a cautious step back.

Errol was confused. What did his mother have against Harley?

"I told you over the phone that I was on a date, mom," Errol explained. "Why are you acting like this for?"

"Do you know who her . . ."

Merle placed his hands on Freah's shoulders to whisper in her ear. Her body was trembling with fire, but his logical theory simmered her rage.

"Sweety, if Teddy Lee knew that he was with his daughter, Errol wouldn't be standing here."

"What's going on?" Errol pressed.

"We can use this," Merle concluded.

This rang true, so Freah quickly said, "Sorry, sweetheart. I mistook you for someone else."

A look of relief washed down Errol and Harley's faces.

"It's okay. I get that a lot," Harley said.

Merle looked squarely at his son and asked him, "Who's ass you kick?"

Errol shook his head. His father had always been a man who believed that, "If you can't beat 'em, pick up a brick and bust their head to the white meat, son. Way of the redneck, ya' hear?" But Errol didn't even accomplish as much as a scratch on them boys, so his father's question made him feel small compared to his six-foot stature.

"He kicked a few asses," Harley answered for him, then went on to explain how her ex-boyfriend, Derrick, and his good-for-nothing brothers jumped on Errol at the gas station.

"Well, by George, they realized quite fast that they done leapt clean down into the eye of a hurricane, I tell ya'. Errol rained down on them boys something fierce, then I grabbed that there rifle of his and told the sumbitches if they don't get, Imma put more holes in 'em than a gopher, by God."

Freah and Merle stared at Harley admiringly, but Errol fell in love with her even more so at that moment. This was what he saw in his parents' relationship while growing up—mutually supportive roles that defined the quality of what a team truly is—togetherness, in which a play-by-play of love is practiced until perfected harmoniously without any interruption. She was his soulmate.

"So how is Uncle Davie doing?" Errol asked, shifting to the dilemma at hand.

Merle took a deep breath. This was hard for him. "If . . . If he makes it—"

"He will," Freah interrupted Merle. "He'll do just that, I tell ya."

Merle drew another deep breath. "He's paralyzed," he said sadly.

Errol's mouth fell open. "What?"

"From the neck down."

Harley looked down at her boots. There was just too much pain flying around.

Errol peppered his parents with a barrage of questions about Davie, Squirrel, Savannah, and Rock-on, in which they were obviously intentionally being vague about it all.

"Rock-on isn't answering his phone?" Errol echoed. "Ain't that a little weird, considering that Savannah—"

Freah cut him off. "Yes, but we don't know what to do. We've called all his little hussies around town, and none of them seen or heard from him. So . . ." She left it at that.

"Sheriff don't know nothing?" Errol asked.

"Does he ever?" Merle said. "But we're gonna go see Squirrel in a bit. Figure he'll fill in a few holes for us."

"But in the meantime, we need you to go with Bella," Freah told Errol. "We'll take Harley home."

"Huh?" Errol and Harley said simultaneously.

"I'm sure your folks are worried sick about you, dear," Freah said. "Late as it is."

Harley couldn't mask her pain, so she quickly lowered her head and said, "It's fine."

But Freah recognized the look immediately—it was a look that she had stared at so many times in a mirror—the pain of the unloved. Due to who Harley's father was, naturally, Freah did not trust her, but in that instant, that very point of her saying, "I'm sure your folks are worried sick about you, dear," she had a sudden change of heart. Teddy Lee and Bobbi had failed to fulfill their daughter's inner needs. This girl was broken—just as she was before Merle saved her. Harley truly didn't know of her father's treachery against their family.

"Give us a minute," Freah told Merle and Errol.

Freah grabbed Harley by the hand and led her toward the door. They were going to have a talk.

The night air was refreshingly crisp and did them both some good. Freah lit a cigarette and looked up at the sky. It had been an extremely long day.

"My ma' and pa' was a piece of shit," Freah said.

Harley looked at her, and while brushing a tussle of her hair behind her ear, she said with a sigh, "Reckon it's contagious."

"Yeah, but it shouldn't be," Freah met her gaze. "So, once this is all over, you're gonna become one of us." She pulled the sleeve of her jacket up and revealed her tattoo.

This baffled Harley.

"Huh?" was all she could say.

"I see the way my son looks at you, and the way you look at him. You two are in love."

"How do you know that?" Harley asked with a hint of amazement.

Freah took a drag from her Marlboro. "Once you've gone without it for so long, yo' begin to recognize it when you see it."

"That's so true."

"And gals like us whose parents don't give a rat's ass about us, belong with this family right here, sugar. Good wholesome folks who will not tell you, but show you every day that you are enough, sweetie. This family saved me, and you're more than welcome to come aboard."

Harley's eyes watered. No one had ever spoken to her like that before. Her father treated her more like a chore, a responsibility that was unwillingly placed upon him—a robotic relationship that seemed rehearsed on his part. But deep down, somewhere, she did feel that he cared. Something was holding him back from loving her entirely, but his blatant disrespect to Holly always seemed to remind her that he may not be her father at all—that something took place that neither he nor her mother wanted to openly discuss with them, or anyone else for that matter. Teddy Lee and Bobbi had always been one foot in, but mostly one foot out, and Harley, for the last time, was fed up with the mess that they had made of themselves, in which she was suffering right along with them—a bloodline of misery.

“I’d like that,” Harley told Freah.

Freah hugged her. “How does it feel?” she asked her. “To feel wanted and loved?”

Harley smiled. The moment felt so right. Freah’s embrace felt so motherly. A tear of joy appeared at the corner of her eye, and she said, “It feels good.”

Chapter 3

Savannah was underneath the blanket, snuggled in his arms. They were smoking a joint while watching an episode of *Breaking Bad*, which was their favorite show.

Freah and Merle were downstairs preparing dinner, so the aroma of savory pork belly and cabbage seeped beneath the crack of the bedroom door. Then thunderous footsteps sounded as a herd of restless children ran past.

"Stop, Errol!" shouted Jaxon.

"Shut your trap!"

"Move, before I tell."

Some dialogue came before Savannah and Rock-on heard the children storm down the steps.

"Baby, it's been four years. When are we gonna get our own place?" Savannah said.

"Soon, honey," was all he said.

"You keep saying that, but—"

"I just wanna make sure we're stable enough to walk on our own, baby, ya' know?"

"We don't need much, Hank," she addressed him by his biological name.

"What's so wrong with wanting to give you the world? You're the gal I'm gonna marry. Let me do this the right way."

Savannah smiled. She was completely in love with Rock-on, so those were sweet words to her ears.

"I would just like to start my life with you before I'm sixty years old."

Rock-on laughed. “By the time we’re sixty, we’ll be living on our yacht, eating cheese and crackers.”

“Eating each other, hell. Fuck that cheese.”

They chuckled.

“At that age, I’ll be lucky to get hard.”

“If we can afford a yacht, we definitely can afford some pills that’ll wake ‘em up for months.”

Rock-on arched his brow. “A hard-on for months?”

“No, years. We’ll have your pants tailored around it. Use it for a step ladder when I can’t reach something in the cabinet.”

The strain of reefer that they were smoking was really good—slanting their eyes and making them silly.

“For a handle,” Savannah continued. With laughter, Rock-on said, “Hot damn, girl, I ain’t got that much wood.”

“Yeah, I was talking about one for a toilet.”

Rock-on’s eyes popped wide at her wisecrack. “Well, I’ll be a monkey’s uncle,” he said, then he bit her playfully on her shoulder.

Savannah giggled and squirmed—he bit her again . . .

. . . Savannah slipped free of her recollection with a smile, then stood up from the kitchen table to retrieve a beer from the refrigerator. On the table were a couple of sticks of dynamite, guns, ammunition, a hacksaw, and several photographs of members of the White Infidels.

***

Rock-on noticed that the car had come to a halt. His eyes were wet with tears, and he was beginning to feel an abnormal dread of being locked inside such close quarters. The trunk was small, like one of a Mazda, as Jaxon currently owned. Rock-on still couldn’t believe that Dog Man had orchestrated a mass attack against the family.

The jingling of keys. Voices. Rock-on began to feel that this was his last ride—that he'd never see his wife and children again.

The lid of the trunk opened. Teddy Lee, Jim Bob, Dog Man, and Jaxon all stared down at him with Wolfish grins. Jim Bob was holding a propane torch in his hand, and Teddy Lee had something like a sword, maybe. The lighting was scarce.

"Well, goddamn, boy, if you do all the crying, what the baby gone do?" Teddy Lee asked.

Jim Bob and Dog Man grabbed Rock-on roughly by his arms and legs, then snatched him out of the trunk. He cried like a defenseless child, but so did Dog Man, who collapsed to his knees in strenuous pain. He was suffering from a case of broken ribs. No thanks to Teddy Lee, of course.

As Teddy Lee and Jim Bob commenced stomping and kicking the living shit out of Rock-on, Jaxon quickly unlocked his Android to video the assault as Teddy Lee instructed, but was careful not to capture their faces—only Rock-on.

A minute passed before Teddy Lee and Jim Bob backed off to catch their wind. Rock-on, a bloody piece of mince meat, was lying on his back sprawled out like a snow angel. He was panting, producing clouds of cold air with every huff.

Teddy Lee placed his boot on Rock-on's arm, then brought the blade of his machete down onto Rock-on's wrist, severing his hand and kicking it under a brush.

Rock-on hollered to the top of his lungs, but the worst had yet to come. Jim Bob triggered the propane torch and applied the blue flame to the open wound—sealing it with hot, stringy flesh.

Dog Man couldn't watch any more of the heinous act. Things were beginning to get well out of hand, which Rock-on no longer had—Teddy Lee chopped off the second one.

This crazy bastard meant business, and there was no stopping him.

While visualizing Errol going through such violence, Jaxon grinned wickedly. He hated his cousin and anticipated the moment when he became the king of Norton High and beyond.

Chapter 4

Merle was talking to his cousin, Bella, in confidence, or so he thought. Errol was standing at a vending machine around the corner listening.

"Jaxon's dead?" Bella said painfully. "No."

"Yeah," Merle said softly.

"In Abingdon?"

"That's who called, yeah. Sumbitch ain't playing fair, I tell ya'. So I need you to watch Errol for me, hear?"

"Okay, yeah, sure, sure."

"Go down to your pa's house and wait for my call."

Bella's father lived in Bigstone Gap, which wasn't very far, but far enough.

Bella nodded. "And the girl?"

"Take her home. The less she knows, the better."

"And what are you gonna do?"

"Imma end this shit tonight."

Freah rushed into the waiting room with Harley close on her heels.

"Merle, my phone and gun have been stolen," Freah said.

"What?" was Merle's reaction. "From the truck?"

"Yeah, and I think it mighta been one of them fuckheads across the street."

Errol walked around the corner with a soda and a candy bar in his hand. "That's easy. Pa', where's your phone?"

Merle patted his pockets, then reached inside his jacket for an inner pocket.

"You and mom are on the same account, so y'all's 'Find My Device' setting is linked as one," Errol explained while tapping his thumbs on the screen of Merle's phone.

Seconds later, he turned the screen around for them all to see. It was a map, and a blip that was the shape of an arrowhead was moving along Cypress Street.

"It's on the move," Errol said.

Merle snatched the phone, and he and Freah ran for the door.

"Pa', charge your phone," Errol yelled, then looked at Bella and told her, "His phone lives on two percent."

"Don't I know it."

Errol grabbed Harley's hand and said with a wink of his eyes, "Heard they got some damn good fiddling in the cafeteria, babes."

"I'm starving," Harley said, stretching her eyes to add emphasis.

Bella looked at the soda and candy bar that Errol had placed on the arm of a chair and figured there must've been some truth to Harley's claim.

"Don't wander off too far, hear?" Bella told them.

Upon exiting the waiting room, Harley asked, "What's going on?"

"That's what Imma find out."

Errol reached into his pocket for his phone as they made their way to the parking lot. If there was one person who could get him the information that he needed, it was his boy Georgie. He knew everything and everyone.

Once they departed the hospital, Harley pulled her hand free of his grasp.

"Errol?"

He looked over his shoulder at her. His phone was up to his ear. "Jaxon's dead," he said.

This took Harley by surprise. Jaxon was a classmate of hers, and although she had categorized him as the biggest jerk-off in Norton, she didn't believe that he deserved to die.

Errol spoke into his phone while hurrying across the lot to his truck. Harley ran to catch up to him and heard him say, "Alright. Call me back as soon as you can."

From the other end of the parking lot, parked at an angle to view the entire perimeter, Derrick and his brothers watched them, and this time they brought their firearms. Errol and Harley were better off dead.

Inside his truck, Errol was transfixed on a ring of thoughts, so they sat quietly. In a matter of no time, their relationship shot to orbit—a grand opening, but also very sad, because someone was targeting his family. Errol didn't believe in coincidences, so whatever was going on was definitely related to Dog Man's murder.

Harley caressed Errol's hand. The people of Norton gave Errol's family a hard ride, but Harley knew that their hate derived from jealousy—a bunch of broke fucks without an idea in the first place. But murder? This situation was downright scary. However, Harley didn't frighten easily. She actually loathed the presence of a prissy bitch who was afraid to get her hands dirty. Harley was a true country gal, bred tough, loyal, and full of fire.

"You okay, hon'?" she asked him, although she knew that it was a stupid question.

Staring through the windshield at a plastic Dollar General bag as it fled with a gust of wind, Errol said, "Reckon they gone kill us all, ya' know?"

"Don't talk like that, Errol," she replied, still caressing his hand.

"My pa' told Bella to take me down to Big Stone Gap."

"What's down there?"

"My pa's cousin, Donnie. Bella's pa'. He got a ranch on the outskirts, freaking no man's land."

Harley wasn't stupid. She said, "A hideout?"

Errol nodded. "Reckon our house ain't safe, which pretty much told me everything I needed to know."

"Which is?"

He looked at her. "I gotta find this guy, and fast."

There was an unnerving glare in his eyes, and although Harley somewhat knew what his answer was going to be, she cut her eyes to the rifle rack and said, "And what are you gonna do when you find 'em?"

His features hardened. "Kill 'em."

Harley's lips tightened. This will change everything. She took a deep breath, then nodded. "In the name of Jaxon."

"No."

Errol was a realist, but he knew that his response came off as a state of reduced sensibility. But truthfully, he didn't give a damn about Jaxon. His cousin had always envied him and was forever trying to oust him in any and everything possible—girls, sports, socially, and even financially—but he had never once proven that he was better than Errol in any category given. Errol used to find Jaxon's jealousy of him amusing, but it was no longer entertaining when their cousin, Jeter, broke into Errol's truck and swiped $400 out of the glove compartment while under the eyes of three surveillance cameras. This unlikely incident called for an ass-beating of unknown origin, and Errol delivered a can of whoop ass, personally.

Two weeks later, while driving to drop his younger sister, Miranda, off at Bella's house for a sleepover, Errol spotted Jeter's old beat-up Oldsmobile at an intersection, and who but Jaxon was sitting in the passenger seat.

"Pa', can I talk to you?" Errol remembered saying to his father that night.

"Sure, son. What's on your mind?"

"Well, I saw a good pal of mine today hanging with Jeter."

"Hmm. Does this pal know that Jeter stole from you?"

"Yeah."

"Then he's no friend you need, Errol. A man who stole from my friend might as well have stolen from me, 'cause that's how imma treat the sumbitch when I see 'em. Smack his goddamn face on his shoulder, I tell ya', by George. Ain't nothing worse than a cross-dresser."

Errol's forehead creased. "Huh?"

"Cross-dresser, boy. A sumbitch who likes to play both sides. Either way, they're tryna fuck ya'."

Errol's phone rang, and Harley saw that it was Georgie calling.

"Georgie," Errol answered.

"Got that information you wanted."

"Hand it over."

"Chicken Hawk been seeing some skank whore down in Pennington Gap. Her name's Amanda Rice, and she works at the Waffle House. Brunette and fat as a hog, from what I'm told."

"You sure about this?" Errol asked skeptically.

"Sure as a man can be, I reckon."

"Alright, thanks, I owe you one."

"Don't mention it. And Errol?"

"Yeah?"

"Be careful. They say this Chicken Hawk fella's a rotten motherfucker, son."

"If he's there, Imma make 'em prove it."

Errol ended the call, then looked at Harley. "Imma take you home, alright?"

Harley crossed her arms over her chest and arched a brow. "Oh, so that's where we're staying tonight?"

This threw him off. "Say what?"

"Oh, I see. You think Imma just let you deal with this shit alone, do you?"

"Harley, this ain't some game. You—"

"Uh, you the one who plays football, sweety. Not me. Games are not in my vocabulary. Now let's go. I heard everything Georgie just said, so Waffle House, here we come." She buckled up. "Bitch better have my eggs and grits."

They laughed.

"Alright, lady, damn."

With a shrug, Harley said, "Together means together. It doesn't mean drop you off at the house and run off to danger, alone, pal."

"Reckon so."

They kissed deep and passionately, then with the turn of the key, Errol pulled out of the lot.

Chapter 5

Walking through the front doors of the Sheriff Department, Patrick paused in his tracks and wiggled his nose as Deputy Brown sped past him, reeking of piss and shit.

"Fucking son of a bitch," Brown grumbled angrily.

Patrick looked at the desk sergeant questionably, who said with a shake of her head, "That goddamn Squirrel back there slinging piss and shit like no tomorrow, I tell ya'."

"I want my fucking phone call!" came Squirrel's voice from the bull pen.

Patrick averted his attention to the corridor to his right that led to the department's detainment unit.

"I'll chop your fucking head off, punk!" Squirrel shouted.

"He likes the sound of his own voice," Sergeant Baines pointed out.

"Most assholes do."

"Be glad when y'all take that sumbitch to Duffield. He's getting on my last nerve."

Norton didn't have a city jail, like most towns in the region, so detainees had to be taken to the southwest Virginia Regional Jail in Duffield—normally within 24 hours of their arrest.

"I'll beat ya' fucking ears shut."

"Where's your pa'? I've been trying to reach him for an—"

"Mama Deans. He wanted to be the one to tell her about Gene's murder."

Sergeant Baines lowered her eyes sadly. "Who could be so mean?"

"No. Who could be so stupid, 'cause pa' gone tear through Norton like a Category Five."

"I sure hope not. Folks ain't gonna take too kindly to Dougherty's brand of punishment."

"No, they're—"

"I want my fucking call!"

Patrick shook his head. "Shut up!" he yelled irritably.

"Come shut me up, faggot."

"That boy bat-hit crazy," Baines said.

Patrick walked around the side of the desk and pushed through a swinging door that led to the central office of daily operations, which consisted of work cubicles, a lab, a booking terminal to process intakes, several offices, and a state-of-the-art break room. Deputies lagged about, killing time—milking the coffee machine to accommodate their chocolate-stuffed crescent rolls. Phones rang, copy machines beeped, and chatter drifted freely from every direction.

Patrick knocked on Maddy Smith's door. She was the data technician, and a mighty damn good one, but he had never cared much for the pompous woman—her approach to self-importance was well over the top. She was either the smartest person in the room or God's gift to men, which she was truly neither.

"Enter," came her high-pitched voice.

"Hey. You busy?" Patrick asked her.

Maddy turned on the wheels of her chair, away from her impressive display of screens and gizmos, saying, "Unlike a lot of you, I actually show up to work, Patrick," then flashed a phony smile and rolled her eyes. "What do you want?"

Patrick closed the door. "Is the system back up?"

"Yes."

"Pop wants you to retrace the racks of this phone." He gave her Freah's device. "It's unlocked."

Maddy's features lightened, which did nothing to heighten her gothic-like appearance. "Great," she said.

As Maddy did her part, Patrick paced the floor, skimming random newspaper clippings that Maddy had framed and hung neatly on the walls. She seemed to admire heroic firemen who had gone beyond the call of duty to save lives.

"Alright," Maddy said.

Patrick looked up at one of the screens and saw the layout of a green map with squiggly yellow lines leading every which way—the tracks.

Maddy lit a cigarette and stood up from her chair to give Patrick a go at it.

He took a seat and quietly studied the map.

"The owner of this phone has been very busy," Maddy said.

"They've been to Duffield."

"Yeah, for a while too."

"Their longest hold over of the night," Patrick said.

As they delved deeper, moving the cursor and distinguishing the red and blue colors that indicated railroad tracks and landscapes, a banner dropped—a text message from a (540) area code.

Patrick and Maddy looked at each other—it was a Roanoke area code, a mountainous city that was over 3 hours away.

"Open it," he instructed Maddy.

Tapping her thumb on the screen of the phone, she saw that it was video, a still image that was way too grainy to make out. The result of a terribly cheap phone.

Maddy pressed the play icon and a painful shriek raced from the speaker of the monitor. They watched in horror as a man wailed from a vicious attack. His lungs croaked for air as the beating persisted. Then the crack of his knee bone made them both briefly look away.

"Jesus," said Maddy.

"Is that . . . I think that's Jack Austin."

Maddy narrowed her eyes. "No. It's Rock-on."

A knock came to the door, and Sergeant Baines walked into the room without first being acknowledged.

"Patrick, Merle and Freah are out front. Said something about tracking their stolen iPhone to this location."

Patrick lowered his head. "Shit."

"Stolen?" Maddy echoed. "Patrick, please tell me you got a warrant for this phone?"

"Not exactly."

Maddy threw her hands up. "Oh my God."

"Listen. Can you store this map and video in a file?"

"Legally, no, illegally, yes."

"Maddy?"

"No, Patrick. Everything that we have here is inadmissible, and I will have no part of it."

"And a gun," Baines said.

Maddy's eyes stretched. "Gun?"

Patrick sighed, then pulled a firearm from his coat pocket.

"Wow. That's textbook shit, right there," Maddy said sarcastically. "No bag or tag here, people," she crossed her arms over her chest. "How exactly did you come in possession of these items, Patrick?"

"I discovered them on suspect," he lied.

Maddy looked at Baines, then back to Patrick. He didn't sound very confident. "And where is this suspect now? 'Cause that's what Merle and Freah are gonna ask you."

"He got away."

"But not before you relieved him of the stolen goods, or turned your body cam on, huh?" She shook her head. "Just doesn't seem likely, deputy."

Maddy was beginning to get on his damn nerves—always by the book. Merle and his family were drug-dealing creeps—who the hell cares?

Patrick addressed Baines. "Tell them that I saw a suspicious-looking character snooping around the Wal-Mart parking lot and recovered the items, but the suspect got away and that I will be out shortly to verify proof of claim. But in the meantime—"

Baines knew where he was going with this and finished his sentence. "Let them visit Squirrel."

"Exactly."

Baines left.

"I don't know what you got going on, but this has danger written all over it, Patrick. Especially that video. Rock-on could be dead because they didn't have their phone to respond promptly."

She was right, and he knew it, but there was no turning back now. "I can't just ignore this video, Maddy."

"No judge will accept it, Patrick. You didn't arrest any—"

"He got away," he shouted.

"Then why didn't you call backup?" she shouted. "Fucking basic protocol, dipshit. You have nothing."

"Madd—"

"Get the hell out of my office before I report you, my damn self."

Patrick looked at the screen. Duffield was the one location at the moment that appeared to be the most promising destination to investigate—if only he had more time to study their routes.

"Out, Patrick," Maddy pressed.

Patrick reluctantly did as he was told, and once he was outside her office, he called his pa'.

"I'm on my way," Dougherty said after Patrick explained their dilemma. "Give them their phone and gun. Maddy gets wet off the thought of burying a corrupt official. So let's just make this go away, fast."

"Got you."

The call ended.

Chapter 6

Freah narrowed her eyes and saw that the exit for Pennington Gap was not far off from that point. The highway was lonely—a long, dark stretch of nothing. Was this a one-way trip? Were Teddy Lee and his nest of cronies lying in wait for blood? What would become of the family after this?

Freah looked up at the moon. She was both mentally and physically exhausted. She knew that things would never be the same after this, but considering all that had transpired, she still hoped for some normalcy, to an extent. Acts of murder have a tendency to haunt the characteristics of a perfectly good soul—a drowning of voices as a tug-of-war, principles and morals battling demons who want the heart, mind, and spirit entirely.

Freah look at Merle, who was riddled with worry—quietly chain-smoking while muddling through that big brain of his. The fact that Patrick was in possession of Freah's gun and phone didn't sit too well with him. He didn't buy Patrick's story one bit. The decorated deputy was hiding something up his sleeve, and there was no doubt in his mind that Patrick had seen the video that the Infidels sent to the phone of Rock-on, but yet he chose not to speak of the footage at all. Suspicions, to say the least.

"Imma give it to 'em," Merle said, breaking the silence.

Freah knew that he was talking about the recipe. "Yeah?" she questioned. "And what's that gonna change, honey?"

He didn't respond.

"Sure. Maybe they'll give us Rock-on and stop attacking us at every fucking corner we turn, but that doesn't make everything fine and fucking dandy, does it?" Her voice cracked. She was on the verge of an emotional outbreak.

Merle looked at his beloved wife. They were hurting . . . bad. And their pain wasn't going anywhere any time soon.

"Dog Man's gone. Jaxon, dead. Davie, Savannah, shot like fucking dogs. Squirrel, locked away, and Rock-on . . ." She broke down. This was her family. The only people who ever gave a damn about her. "Can we really just let this shit go and move on with our fucking lives, Merle?"

"No," he honestly answered.

"Then the only thang we're giving these sumbitches is a bullet."

Merle felt that surge of fire re-enter his heart, and his hand tightened around the steering wheel. Freah was right. Too much had happened to take it all back. He pressed the gas pedal—someone had to die.

Squirrel was able to squeeze Chicken Hawk like a lemon before Davie and him were ambushed from behind. Frightened for his life, Chicken Hawk quickly threw Cunningham under the bus—verifying that he reported to Cunningham and Cunningham only, then gave the Infidels' home address in Pennington Gap. Cunningham was their ticket to Teddy Lee—he was his top enforcer, so if there was anyone who knew where that snake holed up at, it was Cunningham.

Freah needed a cigarette . . . and a bottle of whiskey . . . which she had on hand inside the glove box. She retrieved both.

Swallowing a fiery gulp, Freah made a face as the sting of the alcohol washed down to her stomach, warming the center of her chest in its wake.

"I need to know what's after this, Merle. This life—"

"Isn't worth it," he said. "The benefits don't outweigh the consequences, I know." He took a deep breath. "I got into—"

"I know. To give us a better life." Her voice was soft. "And you have, baby. You've held this family together with sacrifice after sacrifice, and we love you for it, but it's time—"

"To hang 'em up. You're right. I mean, I've been feeling it for a while now, but I just wanted to get my brothers squared away first, ya' know?"

She nodded. "But all they've done is squander every cent on nonsense, Merle. That's not your fault, and you can't keep trying to keep everyone afloat through meth, sweetheart, because our time has obviously run its course."

Freah passed him the bottle. Merle was not a person who was too smart to listen, or just overly opinionated or combative—listening was how he learned whether or not a person was ignorant or not, and his wife was far from stupid. Over the years, he had molded her into him. Silently, they put a dent in the bottle of whiskey—numbing the pain. They both knew that it was time to steer the family in a new direction. The up-and-coming generation deserved better, deserved a chance.

"Reckon we'll buy ourselves one of those RVs, like we talked about," Merle said.

Freah smiled. Hearing this made her heart happy. Her and Merle had dreams of the open road.

"What about Miranda and Rusty?" She spoke of their younger two children. "Who's gonna run our businesses?"

"Reckon we'll homeschool 'em right there on the road," he smiled at the idea. "And it's not like we won't be back to manage our businesses, and whatnot, ya' know?"

She was easily convinced. "I reckon, yeah. That'll work, babe."

"We work."

Her smile widened. "Like a well-oiled machine, huh?"

He nodded, because it was the truth. "Reckon this love for you is what moves me," he told her.

Freah reached for his hand and hooked her pinky around his. "Forever."

"I wouldn't have it no other way."

Merle veered up an exit ramp. A seriousness overtook them both. Freah cocked her pistol. It was time to kick some ass and get Rock-on back.

Then Merle's phone rang. It was his uncle Billy calling him back for the third time in twenty minutes.

"Bill," Merle said, answering on speaker.

"Now, goddammit, Merle, I don't know about this shit here," Billy said in one long breath.

Merle shook his head. "Billy, listen to me. It's—"

"Too soon. We ain't—"

"No, no, it has to be tonight, ya' hear?"

"I reckon you just want us to put it all on the line, huh?" Billy said.

"You goddamn right I do. You two owe me big time, and I—"

"Alright, goddammit. But if we die, I hope your ass burns in hell."

"The last cell in the east end of the building, Billy."

"I know."

"Billy hung up."

"Dumb ass," Merle said.

Freah understood his frustration. Billy and his wife, Robin, weren't the sharpest knife in the drawer. Merle swore to Squirrel that he would get him out of that cell before daybreak, and he never broke a promise.

Freah and Merle went over the details of the jailbreak again, the plan starting to feel like a long shot with Billy and Robin involved. They weren't the sharpest tools in the shed, and it was hard to tell if they'd pull their weight or make everything fall apart.

Beneath the truck, a flickering red light pulsed like a warning, casting their hiding spot in an eerie glow. But who was it meant for? And who else was watching?

Chapter 7

Squirrel paced the small, cramped cell, his mind trying to dig up the name of a halfway decent attorney who wasn't in the judge's back pocket. The air was thick, stifling, and smelled like mold, the heat pressing in on him from every side. Graffiti plastered the walls, and despite the disgust it stirred in him, he couldn't help but read it out of sheer boredom.

'Aryan Pride' 'Johnny was here' 'Lisa Romus's pussy stinks' 'Bring on the meth' 'Fuck Sheriff Dougherty'

Each scrawl seemed to weigh the air down more, like the place itself was suffocating him. "My life is over. Fuck it. Go all the way, Squirrel," he told himself.

Squirrel didn't have any children, nor a particular woman to call his own. He lived life raw and unforgiving, which left no room for whiny children or clingy women. Hell, his loyalty, love, and responsibility to his brothers was enough.

"Squirrel?" came Ronnie Jergen's voice from the neighboring cell.

"What, Ronnie?"

"You ain't got nothin' in ya', do you?"

Squirrel shook his head. People commonly snuck drugs into lock-up by stuffing packages inside their asshole. So, Ronnie's question wasn't entirely out of line—Squirrel just wasn't in the mood for talking.

"Say one more word to me, Ronnie, and I swear for Lord I'ma beat you like a dick when we get to Duffield, boy."

The distinctive sound of the food cart's squeaky wheels filled the corridor, and detainees began to shout through the bars.

"Bout time y'all brought that goddamn food!"

"Lazy-fucks," came a woman's voice.

Squirrel relieved his arm of the sling with a wince. His shoulder ached like hell, but he was famished and wasn't going to attempt to eat with his left hand if he didn't have to.

"Aw, shut it, goddamn lowlifes," said the deputy. "Lucky to be fed at all."

This immediately pissed Squirrel off. He didn't like being talked down to—especially by lawmen.

Meanwhile . . .

Patrick was standing across from the front desk, talking on his phone with his father when Deputy Roberts headed down the corridor with a food cart.

"Yeah, so, from what I could gather in that short amount of time, they were in Duffield for over an hour, pop. On Michigan Avenue, to be exact."

"Hump," Dougherty said thoughtfully.

"So I contacted their sheriff's department and issued a welfare check on every house on that street."

"Good, good, good. Smart, son. Smart."

"Do you really think they killed someone?" Patrick asked.

"Is the sky blue?"

"Actually, no. The reflection of the sun off of the oceans—"

Dougherty hung up.

"Hel-Hel-Hello?" Patrick stammered.

***

Deputy Roberts approached the bars with the cart. He was a frail and lanky man with horrible skin and a large forehead. He was a prick, and Squirrel and him had never gotten along.

Roberts grinned, revealing badly spaced teeth. “Now would yo looka here,” he said, gawking at the bandage wrapped around Squirrel’s head. “Got your ass good this time, didn’t they?” He cackled. “Swell thang too, ‘cause you are an ignorant bastard.”

Squirrel used to terrorize Roberts and his brother, Fennel, in high school and beyond. He even once hog-tied Fennel and tortured him with the intense ray of a magnifying glass in the scorching sun. Fennel cried like a girl on fire.

Squirrel looked down at the tray of food—spaghetti, boiled cabbage, dinner roll, and a pack of peanut butter crackers. Damn, he was hungry.

Roberts saw the yearning for the food in Squirrel’s eyes and seized the pleasure of being the hombre who spat in his pasta. Roberts felt real smug after this—grinning like the cat who ate the canary.

Squirrel didn’t bat an eye. He just simply reached through the slot, grabbed the tray, took hold of the spork, and took a big ol’ bite of that spaghetti.

The deputy was disgusted by this; his facial expression said as much.

“Real men can stomach anything, you fucking bug,” Squirrel said while chewing.

Roberts parted his lips to comment, but his words caught inside his throat when Squirrel dropped the tray and reached through the bars to grab him by the collar of his shirt.

“I hate bugs,” Squirrel growled menacingly, then yanked Roberts' face into the steel, breaking his nose just as the rear wall of the cell crashed in.

Squirrel released Roberts and crouched protectively as dust from the cinder blocks filled the room, causing him to spit and cough.

“Say, boy, brang your ass in!” shouted a voice that Squirrel thought sounded a lot like his cousin Billy.

Squirrel hurried for the opening as the dump truck rolled in reverse.

"Get your ass moving, boy!" came Robin's raspy voice.

Patrick and others ran down the corridor with their firearms extended.

"Roberts?" Patrick said. "What's . . ." Patrick's words trailed off once he looked through the bars of a cell and saw clear out to the parking lot.

"Squirrel," Roberts said, down on a knee.

"Goddamn white boys," Patrick grumbled before running to catch up with the others who were fleeing in pursuit of Squirrel and his co-conspirators.

"Run, Squirrel, run!" yelled the female detainee, laughing.

"Kill that sumbitch," was Ronnie's reaction.

Chapter 8

Amanda Rice walked out the door of the Waffle House and headed to her S.U.V. It's been a long night, more aggravating than anything else, because there were a few customers who nearly caused her to lose her cool and dump a plate of hash browns on top of their heads. It was already bad enough that she was coming down with a cold and had to come in on her day off to fill in for Janice, who was a no-show, again.

A strong gust of wind almost knocked the "To Go" tray out of her hands and she grumbled a complaint. Chicken Hawk wouldn't take too kindly to her coming home without his patty melt hamburger and curly fries, and she sure as hell didn't want to go back inside and have Brad cook another order—she just wanted to go home and take a good hot bath. Plus, it wasn't every day that she got to come home to Chicken Hawk. He was usually wrapped up to the wee hours of the night in his drug business, in which she was usually asleep when he got home, but for some reason tonight he turned in at a decent hour.

The thought of falling asleep in his arms elated her. Men have never taken to Amanda. She was the ugly duckling who never became a swan, which is why she clung so pathetically to the possibility of Chicken Hawk eventually taking her hand in marriage one day.

"Amanda, your butt so flat you need a belt to hold your panties up." "Big girls are only good for one thang, and that's licking the plates before they're placed in the

dishwasher." "Amanda, the Michelin Man called, he said he wanted his neck back." Amanda has heard every insult there is—which toughened her skin—and although she only stood 5'6", she was not fragile by a long shot. She beat skinny prima donna bitches up for fun, and believed in her right to bear arms.

Amanda got behind the steering wheel of her Kia and stiffened as cold air shot from the vents. It normally took way too long for the engine to warm up, and she just wanted to get home, out of the greasy uniform and wedge-riding panties that were driving her insane. So she lit a cigarette, pulled her brown hair free of a ponytail, then pulled out the lot.

Just as Amanda was driving past a number of fast-food restaurants, her phone rang. She didn't recognize the number, but as of late her brother had been making three-way calls from the Duffield regional jail. Surely, he wasn't allowed to call this late, right? He has a lot of important matters to address in his case, so she didn't want to chance missing one of his calls.

"Hello?" she asked.

"You're about to be taken," a voice said.

Amanda crinkled an eyebrow. *Did she just hear this guy correctly? Taken?* "Who is this?" she asked.

The man answered, then said, "Your boyfriend shot some really nasty people tonight, and now their nephew is in Pennington for payback. They tinkered with your engine while you were inside, Amanda."

Amanda looked in her rearview mirror. *They? Was this some kind of joke? Who the hell did Chicken Hawk shoot?* "They're behind you," the man said.

The call ended. Amanda looked in her sideview mirror at a set of headlights that appeared to belong to a truck. Amanda reached to the passenger seat for her purse. Inside was her Glock 17. She had stopped taking crap from people a long time ago—tonight was no different.

Turning left on Cranton Street, the scenery became less glittery than the commercial zone of restaurants and retail stores. Regular businesses such as dental offices, vape shops, and others were closed at this hour, so a darkness lurked on Cranton Street, with the occasional glow of a neon sign.

Then, like the snap of some fingers, her vehicle began to jolt in a spasm-type manner that prompted her to pull over onto the side of the road.

Amanda watched the truck ride past her slowly. It was too dark to make out the faces of its occupants, but it felt sinister. She cocked her gun and eyed the vehicle until it made the turn on Melrose.

Amanda called Chicken Hawk—there was no answer. She tried again—same result, nada. Amanda hammered the steering wheel angrily, then it dawned on her that Chicken Hawk may be . . . dead.

Pulling a latch that unlocked the hood of her S.U.V., Amanda got out to take a look at the engine by the luminous light of her phone.

The black Dodge Ram turned back onto Cranton and pulled over across the street from Amanda. She eased her hand inside her coat pocket and wrapped her fingers around the handle of her gun.

A girl hopped down from the driver's seat. She was ridiculously gorgeous—the type of girl that Amanda has always hated, but inwardly always wanted to be like. From the assistance of the interior lights, Amanda also saw that no one else was inside the truck.

They? Isn't that what the caller said? "They're behind you."

"Hey. Need help?" The girl said.

"Sure," Amanda responded, her voice dripping with suspicion. "You know something about engines and thangs?"

"Yeah," the girl smiled. "My pa's a grease monkey."

"Okay, yeah. Thanks."

The young woman approached the front end of the KIA to take a gander, and as soon as she looked in on the engine, Amanda placed the muzzle of her gun to the girl's temple—feeling her stiffen, all fear and shock rolled into one.

"That man said to tell you that your pa' is really disappointed in you. You know, for dating that—"

The girl struck out, running across the street for her truck and Amanda gave chase, firing a single shot . . .

Chapter 9

Cunningham strapped a belt tightly around his upper arm to shoot up a few ccs of meth. His phone was lying on the coffee table—Teddy Lee was on speaker.

"I just talked to Merle," Teddy Lee said.

"Uh-huh. And what he think about that lil' video?" Cunningham asked, popping his good vein with the needle and pushing the dope into his bloodstream.

"Broke 'em down like a shotgun, son. Sumbitch called me everything in the book, I tell ya'."

Cunningham leaned his head back. He was high as a giraffe pussy. He said slowly, followed with a chuckle. "So what's next?"

"Gave 'em until morning to get that shit boxed up and ready to go, or Rock-On is gonna wake up on the wrong side of the dirt, by God."

Cunningham took a deep breath, feeling an incredible kick of energy. He stood up from the sofa. "Reckon I'll come down in a couple hours, then."

"Hold on, that's Cobra beeping in," Teddy Lee said before clicking over to answer the incoming call, which somehow merged the lines instead. "Yeah, Cobra, what's up?"

"Say, boss, I just got a call from some pussy that Amber knows from Norton. She gave him my number or what—"

"Goddamn, Cobra, get on with it," Teddy Lee said. "I ain't got all—"

"It's about your daughter."

"What about her? She's okay, right? What this guy say? Who the hell is this guy?" Teddy Lee asked, rapid-fire. "Where is she? Imma call her. I gotta go."

"Teddy Lee, wait—hold on. You gotta hear this, bro."

"What? Just say it, Cobra!"

Chapter 10

Merle and Freah were parked down the street from Cunningham's house. The property wasn't much of nothing—a piece-of-shit shotgun house that he had altered by knocking down a few walls and welding two mobile homes to the structure in an uneven fashion, making it more of a visionary eyesore than ever. A disturbing number of cats were walking along the hoods, rooftops, and trunks of a yard full of junkers that were obviously only useful for parts and shelter. Lights burned brightly in the windows—windows covered by sheets that were thin in places and full of holes in others.

Merle passed Freah the joint, then turned the bottle of whiskey up to his lips, anything to refrain from bleak thoughts and exaggerated solutions of closure. He looked for a possible entry point. They were not there to kill Cunningham, but if approached wrongly, their hand could be forced to put his chin in his chest, and doing so would ruin their chance of finding Teddy Lee—the head of the snake.

Billy and Robin successfully broke Squirrel out of jail and torched the stolen dump truck upon swapping getaway vehicles in a vacant lot that was literally around the corner from the Sheriff's Department—catching the deputies with their pants around their ankles. Now the trio was on their way to Pennington Gap to join the hunt for Teddy Lee—it would end tonight.

Freah and Merle finished both the joint and bottle of rye. The street was quiet, a dirt-road community without as much as a stop sign or streetlight. An undeveloped area that relied upon porch lights to verify its existence after nightfall.

Freah chuckled. Reefer had always made her silly.

"You remember," she laughed, and Merle looked at her with *uh-oh* eyes. "Do you remember that night we were making love by that campfire—"

Merle smiled, which felt damn good. "Oh no," he said.

Her laughter mounted. "And that raccoon jumped on you?"

He laughed, but back then it had not been a laughing matter by far. Now that they were reflecting on the incident, it was pretty damn hilarious.

"You were running around screaming like a child," she threw her hands up, laughing her little heart out. "Dick swanging everywhere."

"Damn varmint was clawing me to hell," he said.

"What the dickens was wrong with that motherfucker?"

Extreme laughter.

"Sumbitch was high, I told ya," Merle answered. "Bastard was on Boat."

Love Boat was marijuana that had been soaked in embalming fluid, a psychedelic monster that caused lifelike hallucinations.

This cracked Freah up. "When I ran for help, I came across a house like this one," she pointed to Cunningham's lovely abode. "That *Wrong Turn* type of shit."

"I love that movie."

"A little too much. But babe, when I finally kicked up the courage to knock on the door, those—"

"Here I am being mauled by a jacked-up murderer with fleas, and you're standing there afraid to knock on—"

Laughing, Freah cut him off. "Not fair."

"Not fair my ass."

"*Wrong Turn*, Merle. *The Hills Have Eyes*."

"Freddy Krueger."

Her eyes stretched wide. "Right."

Her expression amused him.

Freah continued. “Very scary business, by George. Very. But I knocked, didn’t I? Came back with some folks.”

Merle laughed at his wife—it was all they could do to keep from crying. Pressure could bust pipes when no outlet was granted—this was their release valve, and although it didn’t feel morally right, it was needed. This was life or death—no amount of pressure could compare to such.

Some headlights turned onto the street and pulled into the driveway of Cunningham’s house.

Freah cocked her gun and said with a giggle, “Dibs on the first sumbitch to be shot.”

Merle’s lip curled into a mischievous grin. “Paper, rock, scissors,” he challenged her.

“Oh, you’re on, pal.”

Hearing the small but loudly malfunctioning engine of the electrical garage door, Merle said in a rushed tone, “That’s our way in. Come on.”

They hopped out of the truck and ran within the shadows. The vehicle pulled into the garage, and as the door was lowering, Freah and Merle rolled past it just before it closed. Freah immediately threw her hand over her nose, then looked at Merle with a sickening expression.

“Shh,” he whispered.

They quickly scrambled behind a stack of boxes.

Chapter 11

The girl struck out, running across the street for her truck and Amanda gave chase, firing a single shot into the air, shouting, "Harley, stop!"

Harley remained on course. Amanda released a second round.

"Stop, or I will kill—"

Errol, lying on his back in the bed of the truck, twisted his torso, rising to an upright position to take aim. His breath caught in his throat, and his finger eased off the trigger of his rifle.

"No, please," he said.

Amanda's arm was wrapped tightly around Harley's throat, a gun shoved to her temple.

"From how I'm told, she's no good to her family no more anyhow," Amanda said. "Y'all think Imma let y'all just kill me and my boy—"

Errol's finger snapped back, and the rifle roared. Amanda's head exploded in a sickening spray, her brains painting the pavement. Harley screamed, nearly jumping out of her skin. Amanda flopped backward like a ragdoll, collapsing dead in the street. Errol didn't flinch. He didn't breathe. He didn't blink.

"Shit," Harley said, gaping over her shoulder at Amanda's body. "Fuck yeah, baby. Hell yeah," She said, gathering her bearings. She felt the heat of that slug as it jetted past her face. "Fucking bitch."

Harley ran to the S.U.V., careful not to leave any fingerprints behind. She yanked the door open and grabbed Amanda's purse—they needed her address. Kneeling down for Amanda's gun, Harley paused, realizing how shaky she was. Murder was goddamn terrifying, but wasn't she just within seconds of killing one of them? Was it not self-defense? Surely, right?

Harley sprinted back to the truck. "Errol? Errol, baby, we gotta go," she said.

Errol was in a trance. He just taken someone's life—for Christ's sake, his dream of being drafted into the NFL was officially over.

Harley slapped him, hard. "Errol, snap the fuck out of it, will ya?"

Errol snapped back to reality, shaking himself free of the trance.

"We gotta go, before someone sees us."

"I got her," he said, hopping down from the bed. "I got her."

Harley kissed him. "Fucking right you did. You got her for me, baby."

They loaded into the cab, and Errol pulled off just as easily as they'd pulled up.

Chapter 12

The faltering flat was a ticking time bomb. The walls and furniture were caked with chemical residue, and stained beakers with Pyrex pots piled on the kitchen counter. The smell in the house was very acidic, even slightly ethereal. Amateurs, Teddy Lee and his boys were mixing any chemical compound they could get their hands on.

Teddy Lee was pacing the living room floor—fingers interlaced behind his back—face tight, jaws set. Harley was not answering her phone, which angered him even more.

Rock-on was bound by rope and locked inside the closet, kicking the door, screaming. “Help. Help. Help.” The smell of his own blood heightened his anxiety. Was he on the verge of bleeding out?

Jim Bob and another gang member named Stark were both sitting on the sofa, watching their boss. The news about Harley dating Errol devastated him. She was now considered trash, damaged goods, degraded, and much more. Teddy Lee had no choice but to put a bullet in her head or have his own gang turn on him—death by execution—a penalty that was set in stone by none other than Teddy Lee’s father. No exemption granted in such.

Dog Man and Jaxon were seated at the kitchen table, well away from the Infidels and their inner politics.

Jim Bob had enough of Rock-on’s raucousness. “That’s it,” he grumbled. “I’m putting a clamp on this bastard.”

He stood up from the sofa and looked around the room for anything useful. Rock-on kicked harder, yelled louder, disruptive as hell. He discovered a large, silver-type wrapping behind the loveseat. Grabbing a roll of duct tape from a shelf, Jim Bob told Stark, "Give me a hand, will ya?"

Teddy Lee called Harley again—no answer. He nearly slung that damn phone to the floor and drove the heel of his boot through it. Why would Harley do something like this?

Opening the closet door, Jim Bob pulled Rock-on out of the darkness by his boots, whereupon releasing him, Stark and he began stomping him in the head and torso.

Teddy Lee called Reah—no answer. Did Merle and she know who Harley was? No. Dirty Merle would've used her for a bargaining chip by now. Teddy Lee had to find out if this accusation was indeed factual.

Jim Bob slapped a strip of tape over Rock-on's mouth, then Stark helped him roll Rock-on's body inside the shiny wrapper and tape the edges to limit Rock-on's movement.

"Alright," Jim Bob said breathlessly. "Grab that end. Toss this sumbitch back in there."

By this time, Teddy Lee was beet red and needed a drink.

Chapter 13

The smell of the garage smacked Freah and Merle in their faces fiercely, like dookie on a stick, steamy shit stew, a shit-a-thon so potent they could taste it.

A cute middle-aged woman got out of the car and opened the back door. They saw that she worked at Wal-Mart and was with child, an adorable little boy with frosty blonde hair and a dry smudge of chocolate on his cheek.

"We're home, little man," the woman said sweetly. "Get you a bath, huh?"

The boy giggled as she unfastened the buckles of his car seat.

"Your Elmo pajamas, you say?" she teased him. The boy was still in the goo-goo-gah-ghah stage. "We'll see," she said.

Watching the lovable exchange between mother and son, both Freah and Merle inwardly knew that they weren't going to harm them.

The garage was a dump with piles of moldy clothes, garbage, and decayed rats. Two doors—one led into the house, the other led outside.

The woman entered the house with the boy in her arms, balanced on her hip.

Shaking her head, Freah said, "Uh-uh, hell no, fuck this." Then she stood up from behind the boxes to head to the door for some fresh air. "I'll be in the truck."

Merle stopped her. "Nope," he said, snickering at her wild-eyed expression. She was holding her breath.

"Do you smell that? Somebody needs to wipe their ass."

"Like, all day," he joked. "Just sit down and wipe their life away."

This made her smile.

"With a blanket," she said. "Wipe their ass with a blanket."

Merle stepped toward the door with his shotgun extended. "And the sheet," he said from over his shoulder.

"Where the fuck you been?" they heard a man shout upon Merle easing the door open.

***

"Where the fuck you been?" Cunningham snapped.

Ginger flinched. "Work," she managed to say.

"Bitch, you got off forty minutes ago."

Ginger's eyes cut toward the front door. She considered making a run for it. Whenever Cunningham was hopped up on meth, he became paranoid and extremely violent.

"I had to pick Tyler up from momma's, then—"

"Shut up. Damn town only so big, bitch. What the—"

She cut him off. "Why are you so mad? I didn't do anythang."

Cunningham's face tightened. "Put him down," he told her.

Ginger was no fool. She knew that he was intending to strike her—he enjoyed fucking up her day, her life.

"Why? I got him. He's—"

Cunningham punched her in her face, and she staggered into the wall, but her hold on Tyler didn't falter.

"Bitch, what I say?" he yelled.

Ginger wept. "I didn't do anythang."

Cunningham snatched his son from her and tossed him onto the floor.

"Tyler!" Ginger wailed.

The boy cried painfully.

Cunningham grabbed Ginger by her throat and squeezed so tightly that the whites of her eyes instantly turned red. Shoving his free hand down the front of her pants, he plopped his middle finger inside her pussy, swirled it around a bit, then yanked his hand up to his nose for a whiff—sweaty.

Cunningham released her, and she collapsed to a knee, thirsty for air.

“Get your stinky ass in the shower, bitch.”

Ginger scooped Tyler up into her arms and hurried out the room. Cunningham watched after her, and just as she disappeared around the corner of the hallway, the butt of a shotgun crashed into the back of his skull with amazing force. A sickening crack sounded in his ears, and he fell face-first onto the floor—breaking his two front teeth and nose upon impact.

“Reckon we’ll stick something in you to see where you been,” said a woman.

Cunningham drifted to unconsciousness, but then the bitterness of a blade pierced his calf and brought him back awake. He groaned painfully.

“As I was saying,” came the woman’s voice again. Then a strong pair of hands grabbed hold of his shoulders and rolled him over onto his back.

His vision blurred, watery and unfocused.

A pulsing ache radiated from the back of his skull and down his calf, sharp like a blade shoved deep.

Blood poured from his nose, dripping into his throat, thick and warm, choking him with every ragged breath.

“You’re gonna show us everywhere you been, you piece of shit,” the woman told him. Then the blade punched into his thigh with a twist.

Cunningham parted his lips to scream, but a meaty hand covered his mouth before he could do so, then socked him in his gut.

"I'm not your equal or your playmate, boy. So I reckon you talk," a man growled, his words thick with menace. Cunningham could taste the sour sting of liquor on his breath, the harsh bite of reefer and tobacco in his clothes. He could feel the violent hunger in the air, the murderous energy of the two assailants pressing down on him like a weight.

"Let's get him up and out," said the man.

Then, out of nowhere, Cunningham saw the butt of a shotgun slam down onto his forehead, and darkness closed in on him fast.

Chapter 14

"It was a set up, Errol, I'm telling you," Harley said. "That bitch said as plain as day, 'That man said to tell you that your pa' is really disappointed in you.' She was expecting us."

"And that's your pa' calling your phone right now?"

"Yeah, like crazy. She also said something or another about me dating, but by that time I was getting ready to run."

Errol looked at the speedometer to make certain that he wasn't going over 65 mph. The address on Amanda's driver's license was added to his GPS, and their estimated time of arrival was exactly 8 minutes from now.

"Definitely weird," Errol said. "Reckon she knew we botched her engine and all."

"But how? Georgie was the only person who knew we were coming down here."

Errol didn't like the sound of that. He looked at Harley. She was insinuating that his friend had betrayed him.

"Maybe he told someone," he said. "Someone who knows your pa'. Which is why Amanda said that to you."

"Well, we need to know who this someone is, because I know for a fact that if Amanda knew my pa' personally, she would've never put a damn gun to my head, bygeorge. Someone's playing puppet master with our fucking lives."

Errol had to consider Harley's theory, but why would Georgie sail them up shit creek with no paddles? What does he gain by doing so?

Errol reached inside the console for his phone.

"Who you calling?"

"Georgie."

He put it on speakerphone.

"Hey, what's up, bub?" Georgie answered on the third ring. He sounded as though he was maybe asleep, or high—most likely high, knowing him.

"Aye. Did—"

"Son, where are you?" Georgie interrupted, a newly found pep now in his voice. "Are you watching the news?"

Errol looked at Harley. This was it. Someone saw him kill Amanda. The authorities found the shell casing with his fingerprint on it, and Georgie was about to tell him that his and Harley's photographs were plastered on the screen.

"No, why?"

"Your fucking uncle broke out of jail, son."

Harley was holding her breath—relieved, she released a gush of air and allowed her eyelids to close for a brief moment.

"You're kidding?" Errol said.

"Shitting me. That motherfucker's a goddamn god, son," Georgie laughed. "Sumbitch long gone."

"How'd he—"

"Some crazy motherfucker drove a fucking truck through the wall. They ain't taking that sumbitch alive, I tell ya'."

"Damn," was all Errol could say.

Georgie relayed the details of the jailbreak in further extent. Squirrel was officially a Norton Legend, but Errol knew that there was no happy ending for his uncle—maybe even for them all.

"Listen. Amanda Rice?" Errol said.

"Uh-huh?"

"Did you tell anyone?"

"Hell no, son. Why would I do that for?"

Errol and Harley shared a look. They didn't completely believe him, but he was Errol's right-hand man, so he had to maintain some degree of faith in his boy.

"Okay, well, where'd you get the information from?" Errol asked him.

"Derick."

Both Errol and Harley's mouths fell open, and they said simultaneously,

"Derick?"

"What? Did he make Amanda up, or something?" Georgie wanted to know.

"Georgie, that bastard wants me dead," Errol said.

"What? Why?"

"Harley."

"Harley? That relationship was over before it even started," Georgie pointed out.

"He's obsessed with me," Harley said. "Like, bad-bad."

"Him and his fucking brothers just jumped me," Errol told him.

"What!" Georgie exclaimed. "Don't be playing with me, Errol. 'Cause I'll beat 'em blue, son." Anger was laced throughout his words.

"Not if I get to 'em first."

"Now it's making sense," Harley said. "He gave up Amanda, then gave Amanda the heads up 'bout my pa' and all, by George. Sneaky little fuck, I tell ya'."

"But he told me he didn't know her, just that he heard about her through the grapevine and thangs, ya' know?" Georgie said.

"Yeah, but it wouldn't have been nothing for him to call the Waffle House and speak with her, or even get her number, somehow," Harley stated.

"But why? How does doing that affect you?" Errol said. "Reckon he's aiming for the situation to take care of me. He wants me out of the picture."

Errol had an incoming call. It was his cousin Billy.

"George, that's Billy calling. I'll call you back," Errol told him, then clicked over to the waiting line. "Billy?"

"Boy, where the hell are you at?"

Errol wrinkled a brow. “Squirrel?” he said, recognizing his uncle’s voice.

“Your mama in the hospital down in Pennington Gap.”

Errol’s breath caught inside his chest, but he managed to say, “What? What happened?”

“They were—”

A gunshot cracked like a whip, and the rear window shattered. Harley yelped and lowered her head protectively as Errol fought to regain control of the wheel. The truck skidded left, right, left, right. *Skirt, skirt, sciiirrr!* Smoke wafted from the back tires that left black marks in its wake.

With half of his body suspended out of the passenger side window of Curly’s truck, Derrick took another shot with his rifle.

“Harley!” Errol shouted.

***

Previously . . . In Slow Motion

In the moment of these four events, the Heavens parted, and the most beautiful—saddest instrumental that one could ever imagine played softly in the background of these series of shots.

Merle sped through the streets of downtown Pennington with a cigarette balanced between his lips. Freah, facing Merle from the passenger seat, was showing him the screen of Cunningham’s phone. There were text messages from the same number that Teddy Lee had been calling her phone from, and one in particular was instructing Cunningham to use his wife’s credit card to order some food from Cracker Barrel and DoorDash it to 6349 Cayman Street. There was only one Cracker Barrel in Southwest Virginia, and it was in Lee County.

Merle looked in his rearview mirror at Cunningham, who was lying in the back seat unconscious. They were en route to a nearby rock quarry, because although they were certain that they had finally pinpointed Teddy Lee's current whereabouts, Cunningham still needed to be disposed of—one less Infidel to worry about.

That persistent red light was still blinking in the undercarriage, and the tracker was hanging three cars back in a black sedan. It was none other than Sheriff Dougherty, who was out of uniform and packing his personal revolver. He was not a lawman at the moment, but a vigilante.

***

Medical experts were running down the corridor to Savannah's room. Her condition had taken a turn for the worse, and her vital signs were declining dramatically.

"Oxygen, now. We're losing her," ordered Dr. Weslin, working feverishly to save his patient's life.

"Her blood pressure's dropping," said one nurse who was preparing an injection.

***

Rock-on lay inside the dark, musty closet, suffering internal damage from the beating that Jim Bob and Starks had given him moments ago. His brain was hemorrhaging, slowly swelling and distorting his train of thought, fogging his memories. He was crying, mumbling his wife's name behind the strip of duct tape that was securely over his mouth, because he could feel it—he was dying.

***

With his phone up to his ear, Teddy Lee walked past Dog Man and Jaxon, who were seated at the kitchen table playing Gin Rummy.

"Hey, this is Harley. Sorry I missed your call, but—"

Teddy Lee kicked a trash bin over, startling Dog Man and Jaxon, prompting Jim Bob and Starks to drop their meth pipes and reach for their guns on the coffee table.

Teddy Lee flipped out into a violent fit of rage, smashing glass beakers and prex's, kicking holes in the lower cabinets, punching dents in the refrigerator doors.

***

Cunningham's eyes snapped open, then they bounced around in search of familiarity as his brain swatted the cobwebs that frosted his memory. But upon settling his peepers on Merle behind the steering wheel of the vehicle, it all came back to him. Scenery whizzed past the windows with the yellow glow of the streetlights.

Without a second thought, Cunningham lurched up from the seat and attacked Merle. The truck swerved dangerously through an intersection and was T-boned by a speeding vehicle. The truck tumbled into another car, spun a 360 on its side before smacking a curb and propelling through a storefront window.

***

Beep, beep, beeeeeepp!

Savannah flatlined.

Medical did their best and exhausted all of their remedies, but there was just no saving her.

Savannah was gone.

***

With the memory of their family trip to Daytona, Florida, Rock-on cherished the moment when their oldest daughter, Minny, received her first unwanted gulp of ocean water at the beach. The look of pure disgust was hilarious, but the scratching of her tongue was completely side-splitting.

Rock-on managed a small grin before taking his last breath. He didn't get a chance to make it right, to correct his wrongs, but loss is a part of it, because the drug game is a venomous bitch.

***

Teddy Lee plopped down onto the sofa and took a huge hit of meth from a customized pipe that read: "Ice Ice Baby."

Harley was dead to him.

***

Back to the Present

"I'm okay . . . I'm okay, babe," Harley said while wiping blood from her cheek. The bullet grazed her. Derick was really aiming to kill her.

"Run, you motherfuckers!" Tatum shouted. He was standing in the bed of Curly's truck with a heavy-duty rifle.

"How is this asshole finding us?" Errol said, pushing 90 mph.

Harley returned fire, the powerful rifle clapping thunderously in the cab of the RAM.

"I don't know, it's like . . ." Harley's words drifted as it dawned on her. The conversation at the hospital about Freah's phone. "Shit," she murmured.

Bullets tagged the RAM with a *ping*, *ping*, *ping* effect. Then Curly rear-ended them, causing Harley to fall against the dashboard and lose hold of the rifle.

Errol looked at her, then ducked a stream of incoming bullets. The RAM swerved to the left lane.

"Fuck," he cursed.

The smell of rubber mingled within the folds of cold, aggressive wind. This had abruptly become the highway to hell.

"Them dogs on ya' ass, boy," Tatum yelled, firing his weapon.

Harley took aim.

"Shoot, goddammit, shoot!" Errol shouted.

"Them dogs ain't gone hunt, son," Harley hollered, pulling the trigger, hitting Tatum square in his chest. Then, quickly redirecting her aim, she plucked the trigger again.

The front tire of Curly's truck popped loudly, and the truck flipped forward, sending Tatum sailing through the air. Derrick held on for dear life, eyes wide with fright.

Then—

Whoooom!

A fiery ball of wreckage tumbled down the highway behind the RAM. Flaming items flew forward, upward, backward, and outward—landing with a *clang*, *clang*, *cling*, *cling*, *ding*, *ding*, clomp!

Errol cut left, right, avoiding raining debris.

"Look out," Harley shouted.

Chapter 15

Errol turned onto a dirt road and slammed his foot on the brake. Dust stirred and danced amongst the beams of the headlights. He got out of the truck and walked away, then turned around and walked back to the truck, only to walk away again. He was in shambles.

"They're dead, I know it, I fucking know it," he said.

Harley hopped down from the back. She was feeling the pressure of murder as well, but she understood that it had to happen. Derrick orchestrated their encounter with Amanda's death; he intended to use it against them if all else failed. Derrick and his brothers were a liability that she wasn't willing to gamble on.

"Babe, there was no other way," she said.

Errol looked at her. His heart and mind were racing at 100 mph.

"If he couldn't kill us, he'd've told on us. Anythang to keep us apart."

"Yeah, I get that, Harley, and you're right, but it's just so much. I play ball. You're a cheerleader. This ain't who we are."

"I know, or at least I thought I knew."

Errol didn't understand.

"What you mean?"

Harley shrugged.

"Reckon one doesn't know who they are until they know what they're capable of, ya' know?"

She had him there.

"And I know how they've been tracking us."

"How?" he wanted to know.

Harley held up her iPhone.

"This."

"Huh?"

"When we were together, he bought it for me, put me on his plan and thangs."

"Your location's on?"

She looked down at her cowboy boots shamefully.

"Not something that I really thought about. Sorry."

Errol parted his lips to speak, but then it hit him. The exchange about her phone reminded him about the call from Squirrel.

Patting his pockets, he said, "Shit."

"What is it? What's wrong?"

"My phone."

He ran to his truck.

Chapter 16

"Ma'am, I would advise against this," Dr. Kellerman told her. "Because although we've successfully popped the joints back in place, the extent of your injuries call for surgical screws and therapy, to say the least."

Robin looked at Freah, whose arm was in a sling, and said, "Maybe you should listen to her."

Freah, staring at them through swollen slits, said sternly, "I'll be fine."

"No, you won't," said Kellerman, a stout, broad-shouldered brunette. "If that leg of yours isn't set correctly, it'll give you problems from here on out."

"My husband needs me."

"He'll manage."

"We don't manage too well without each other," Freah countered, then looked at Kellerman's gold wedding band. "Given that you're married, I figured you'd know as much, doctor."

Kellerman looked at her wedding band with a questionable glare—although married, this woman didn't know the first thing about unity. Her yearning expression stated as much.

Kellerman knew nothing of the current dilemma—Merle was taken, and Freah was the only discovery upon the moment when emergency personnel arrived at the crash site. There was no evidence recovered in the wreckage. Cunningham saw to that, taking their guns and Freah's purse, and had he not assumed that she was dead instead of unconscious, Freah was certain that he would've surely planted a slug in her cranium.

Kellerman sighed and tucked her clipboard underneath her arm. "Alright, well, make sure to sign out, and hopefully, you'll return after helping our husband do whatever he's doing," she said with a smile. "Have a goodnight." She took her leave.

Freah limped to the restroom to get dressed. She was in bad shape, but there was no time to lay down and lick her wounds. Teddy Lee was most likely in possession of Merle by now, and she knew exactly where to find him.

Once Freah was inside the restroom, she let her gown fall from her shoulders, then carefully eased down onto the toilet to pull her blue jeans on.

"Ah." She winced painfully.

"There was nothing elaborate about this escape, John," Freah heard an anchorwoman say on the television as Robin upped the volume.

Instinctively, Freah paused and cut her eyes to the restroom door—listening intently to the broadcast.

"The masked culprits simply crashed through this wall that you see behind me," said the reporter, John. "Ditching the stolen dump truck almost immediately after the break, Tammy. This was just too simple, and heads are surely to roll by morning at the department."

Freah slowly stood up from the toilet and pulled her jeans up to her waist with a painful grimace on her face. She had Billy and Squirrel on standby. Freah felt fortunate to have Squirrel at her side. She loved all of her brother-in-laws, but Squirrel had always been her favorite one, and with the intensity of the situation they were in, his brand of 'CRAZY' was just what the doctor ordered.

Freah didn't bother with unfastening her sling to get her arm through the sleeve of her shirt; she just simply pulled it down over the support bandage. Staring at her battered features in the mirror, Freah began to cry. She couldn't fathom life without Merle. She felt empty and powerless—an extreme sense of heartache, but also guilt-ridden because the thought of her children should provide her with all the might to topple the Infidels, but it didn't. She needed her better half.

"Hey, sweety," Freah heard Robin say.

"Hey, Robin. Where's my momma?"

It was Errol. He rushed to his mother's aid. This warmed Freah's heart.

"What happened? Where's my pa'?"

"They took 'em. Some goddamn fool named Teddy Lee got 'em."

Freah shook her head and reached for the door handle—Robin talked too damn much for her liking. Always has. Bitch.

"Teddy Lee?" Harley said the instant Freah swung the door wide. "That's my dad."

***

Meanwhile . . .

Sheriff Dougherty drove through a residential neighborhood with the annoying racket of his captive, who was being disruptive inside the trunk.

Dougherty turned his radio on, then reached for his can of Skoal in the passenger seat.

***

Cunningham turned into a dark wooded area with the annoying racket of his captive, who was being disruptive inside the trunk. Pulling to a halt in a vast clearing of sticks and pine cones, he killed the engine. Here is where it all will end.

Cunningham cocked his pistol and got out of the car with a wince—he was battered and bruised, but his well-being was of no immediate concern—not anymore.

Chapter 17

"Your dad?" Robin echoed. There was a look of danger in her eyes.

Freah quickly intervened before things escalated. The shockingly discombobulated look on Errol's face was concerning, but Harley was just as throwed off as he was.

"Your pa' killed Dog Man and Jax—"

"Robin, shut the hell up, will ya?" Freah snapped.

Robin stomped her foot irritably, but clamped shut because Freah was not the one to piss off.

"Mom, what's going on?" Errol said carefully.

Freah sighed. This was a matter of bad timing, but it had to be addressed for the sake of these two kids who were dealt a crummy hand. Freah knew all about holding such cards, so she couldn't cheat her son out of an explanation that was part of the shuffle, but she had to be tight and clear, because there wasn't much space between this and the window of time that they have to rescue Merle.

"The White Infidels have forged a war against us, and—"

With a foggy expression, Errol cocked a brow and said, "The White who?"

Harley looked at him but didn't comment. Her grandfather was the founder of the biker outfit that she had always disassociated herself with—she disagreed with their standard beliefs of hate and purification of the country by eliminating people of color.

"Infidels," Freah said, shifting her eyes to Harley. "Bikers, run by her pa'. They're steering to wipe us all off the table, and—"

"So far they're doing a pretty damn good job," Robin interjected. "Got us hiding left and right, I tell ya'."

"Hush," Freah looked at her evilly.

"Why are they doing this?" Errol wanted to know.

Freah took a deep breath. "Drugs."

"They want the whole damn pie," came Robin's input.

"But that's only part of it. Your pa' and her pa' used to be friends until a deadly misunderstanding drove them apart."

Freah told them the story, sparing them no details of the chain of events that led up to Bobby Dupree's pregnancy, which actually put a lot of things in perspective for Harley, especially about her sister, Holly, and their abnormal birth.

"My mom cheated," Harley said, more to herself with a thoughtful expression. "No wonder my pa' hates her so much."

"Can't blame 'em any," Freah said. "It's just that Merle never betrayed your pa', Randy did," she winced painfully. "But he has never known the truth, so naturally, he hates Merle."

Errol helped his mother to the sofa, easing her down alongside Robin, who was shaking her foot to calm her anxiety.

"Why did ya'll keep this from me?" Errol asked her.

Freah's expression saddened. "Cause we saw that you loved her, and at that point, so did we."

Freah's revelation rocked the core of the two teenagers, creating pools of water in both of their eyes.

"In order for you two to be given a chance, we had to protect you from this fight, and the best way to do that was to keep ya'll in the dark and hope for the best."

Harley's tears spilled over the rims of her eyes. "But my pa' killed—"

Freah cut her off. "We don't choose our parents, sweetheart. What he has done is solely his to own up to, not yours."

"Talk about a rock and a hard place," Robin said to Harley. She obviously disliked her.

A nuke had just been launched into the lovebirds' atmosphere, targeted to destroy their future together. What kind of shitty, fly-by-night bullshit luck was this?

They all spoke further. Freah told them about the accident that landed her in the hospital and Merle within the jaws of a shark.

"My pa's been calling me like crazy. I'm pretty sure he knows about Errol and me now."

Freah made a face. "Which he will never condone."

Robin shook her head and said, "Everyone knows the Infidels hate black folk. It's always been that way."

Errol and Harley looked at one another. The likes of interracial couples were frowned upon in the traditional areas of southwest Virginia, but Harley was colorblind—so was Savannah, who was disowned by her family for choosing to be with Rock-on. Lisette sacrificed her bloodline for Dog Man, receiving the well-renowned tattoo that so many women in Norton sought after, 'White Girl,' after officially exchanging marriage vows with one of the white boys: Merle White, Davie White, Errol White, and so on. Merle was the only brother who had never dated outside of his race—Freah was a magnificent chocolate drop.

Black rednecks.

Robin's phone chimed. It was a text message from Billy.

Billy: Hon', what's the hold up? We're wasting time here.

Robin looked at Freah and said, while brushing a strand of her blonde hair away from her face, "Freah, we gotta go, sugar."

"Go. Go where?" Errol questioned, wiping his eyes dry.

"Get your pa' back," Freah answered.

"And Rock-on," Robin added.

"Mom, you're in no shape to go anywhere."

"I lose your pa', I'll never be in shape again, Errol."

Harley and Robin both lowered their heads thoughtfully—the strength of love was admirable, and they inwardly favored her response.

"Get back to Norton and do as Bella says," Freah told Errol.

"But mom, I—"

"I don't want to hear it, and I won't tell you again."

Errol sighed. He wasn't prone to back talk and normally did as his parents instructed him to do, but this was not a matter of curfews or homework; this was a whole different ball game.

"Okay," he lied. "But you need to be careful."

"No. They do."

Chapter 18

James, Gene, and Sammy ran throughout the prairie, catching fireflies inside their mason jars. Their family farmhouse was just beyond the hill, and the faint call of their mother's sweet-sounding voice hardly carried the distance. Dinner was on the table and they dared not keep their pa' from making grace.

"Come on 'fore pa' see our hide," James told his younger brothers.

The Dougherty boys ran for the hill, holding tightly onto their jars so not to drop them in their haste to make it home. Sammy was the fastest of the three, so he was way ahead of James and Gene—laughing as he called them such names as, 'slow pokes', 'girly legs', and 'lazy louts'.

"I'll show you a slow poke, you jip!" James said, arms pumping like pistons, skinny little legs chugging with all of their might, but he couldn't catch Sammy.

Grass whipped at their bare ankles, and their trampling stirred the aroma of manure patties. James and Gene were side by side at this point, laughing with curiosity of who was going to arrive at the house in second place.

"Not today," Gene said breathlessly.

"Not today or tomorrow," James countered.

The moon was beginning to take effect as night slowly crawled forward with the announcement of crickets. Summers on the Dougherty farm was always adventurous for the boys, and today was no different. Their tree house that was just west of the lake that behind the house harbored the water moccasin and muskrat that they captured today. The brothers usually set out early in the morning to conquer the land, but never spoiled the opportunity to have fun stick fights, water fights, shooting expeditions—a courageous, highly competitive bunch.

Then.

Gene lost hold of his jar and slid to a halt to retrieve his fireflies.

James also stopped, asking Gene, "Did it break?"

Flashing his snaggle-tooth grin, Gene said, "Nope," then took off running.

"Cheater," James shouted, and that's when it happened.

The unthinkable.

The initial shudder of the earth caused Gene to stumble, crashing face-first onto the ground, landing on top of the jar that shattered violently. James struggled to maintain his balance as the ground rippled beneath his feet. Then, with the thunderous sound of a falling tree, the earth cracked open, wide and deep—swallowing Sammy whole.

"Sammy!" James cried.

James ran to his brother's aid but more ground collapsed from beneath the prairie, hindering his approach. In a panic, James grabbed Gene by his ankles and pulled him away from the edge of the growing chasm, but as he did, shards of glass lodged deeper into Gene's abdomen.

"Ahh!" Gene cried in agony.

"James!" came their mother's voice, frantic.

James looked up just as his parents burst out the door, rushing to help, but they barely made it off the porch before the house itself crumbled and vanished from sight, swallowed by the vast sinkhole. Moments later, the lake's waters gushed in, flooding the hole on top of them.

"No!" Both Gene and James screamed in horror . . .

. . . Dougherty pulled free of that memory with a tear. His family didn't resurface, leaving only Gene and him to mourn the unfortunate tragedy. And now Gene was gone, killed by Dog Man and his coconspirators, and they were all going to die a terrible death for what they did. Since the discovery of his brother's death, Dougherty had been having unexplained crying spells, fueled with agitation and frantic anxiety attacks. Gene had his problems, but he didn't deserve to have his fucking face and head bashed in like a can. An intense feeling of guilt and self-condemnation plagued the lawman. Deep down, he knew that he could've done more for his brother, and if he had, this may not have happened.

Fuck!

Fuck!

Fuck!

Fuck!

Fuck!

The curses poured out a million times over, but none of them could ease the crushing weight of regret for all the times he ignored his brother's cries for help. Dougherty had failed him, and now, he had to make things right. Turning onto the long gravel road that led to Dog Man's house, Dougherty killed the headlights and navigated by moonlight at a moderate speed so as not to alert anyone of his arrival. He had been in law enforcement for a great deal of his 50 years of living and there was one thing that he always saw—fugitives couldn't help but to either return to the scene of the crime or to their house. People have a difficult time parting with their loved ones and their personal belongings.

The house was dark. There was no sign of life and Dougherty wondered where Lisette and the kids were at, at this hour. He pulled over and watched the property. Dog Man and Jaxon didn't have a clue that they were made, so there would be no reason for them to be on edge, but Dougherty learned a long time ago when he was just a patrolman that one could never be too careful.

"*Umph, umph, umph,*" came the muffled pleas of his captive inside the trunk.

Dougherty got out of the car to listen. Sounds were useful when hunting, as were smells. He took a strong whiff of the nippy air that awoke his lungs, hoping to pick up the trace of cigarette smoke or cologne, maybe. This would be his post, his tree barracks as he lay in wait for blood. The contacts of this house held the answers to why this all happened. Why was Gene targeted of all people?

Dougherty and the department had launched an extensive investigation against the White Boys and their meth empire—orders handed directly down from Mayor Applegate, personally. And on several occasions, when they raided a location, they recovered mountains of money and meth that belonged to the whites. So maybe this was payback for costing them hundreds of thousands of dollars in proceeds. Dog Man's little way of saying, "Fuck you, too."

But James Dougherty would have the last "fuck you." Dog Man was his kill.

Dougherty walked to the rear of the car and unlocked the trunk. The interior light flickered before stabilizing. Merle, gagged and bound by zip ties, stared up at Dougherty angrily.

Kidnapped.

"Can't snag a snake without a berry now, can we?" Dougherty said with a menacing smirk.

Chapter 19

Cunningham leaned against the car and lit a cigarette—gun in hand. Murder was an acquired taste, but he'd had a stomach for it since he was a boy in Lee County. It was a trait that drew the attention of the Infidels, but as a result of having the knack to draw blood, Cunningham had spent a substantial amount of time behind bars. At this point, though, he was tired. Life's woes had steamrolled over him twice already, but tonight was the last straw.

Cunningham looked up at the sky, spotting both of the dippers. He thought about his mother—the one person who truly gave a damn about him. After being diagnosed with Inflammatory Bowel Disease, his mother became septic, which ultimately claimed her life. Cunningham would never forget that wristband the hospital had placed on her, the letters (DNR)—Do Not Resuscitate. There wasn't a son out there who could fathom such words being placed upon their mother. Seeing that wristband that morning crushed the little hope he had left for her survival.

Cunningham hadn't put much thought or energy into the idea of a god, but tonight he wondered if all that gibberish his mother used to talk about when he was a boy was true. Was there some mysterious being overlooking it all? Answering prayers while igniting wildfires and manifesting miracle births all at once? A devil? A burning incinerator for corrupt souls? Cunningham doubted as much, but if by chance it was all true, he sure would like to see his mother again. She had a way of making him feel as though everything was going to be all right, and tonight, he needed her voice and wisdom to save himself from himself.

He had never understood love. His father would swear to his right hand that he loved his wife's dirty bathwater, but then turn around and beat her black and blue. One would suspect that after growing up in an abusive household, as Cunningham did, he wouldn't dare think to lay his hands on a woman, but it was the complete opposite.

"Your pa' gotcha thinking that's how you control a woman, but it's not," his mother once said when she caught wind that he'd smacked his girlfriend at the time. "You treat her right and she's gonna do everythang you asked her to do, and then some."

Cunningham didn't grasp his mother's advice that day, and he was arrested two weeks later for domestic assault on a spouse of a family member.

"Cunningham, please don't do this," cried Ginger from inside the trunk. "I'm sorry. I wanna go home. Let's go home, baby."

Ginger and their son were both crying hysterically, and it pained his soul to listen to them.

"Shut up," he shouted. "Shut up." He ran to the trunk and kicked the bumper. "Shut the fuck up!"

"I'm sorry," Ginger blubbered . . .

. . . Cunningham steered the stolen car up through Cypress Hallow, a windy, narrow road with very little scenery or houses. He called Teddy Lee's phone again—still no answer. Cunningham was certain that his boss was currently emotionally attached to the situation with his daughter. Harley had overstepped her bounds by not only dating a black boy, but a boy who belonged to her father's long-time rival, Merle White. Their outfit was totally against mixing races, especially with blacks, and although Cunningham completely understood the sensitivity of it all, in his opinion, now was not the time to focus on Harley and her outlandish behavior. The job at hand should be at the forefront of all their agendas.

Cunningham was leaking terribly from several wounds, but going to the hospital in Pennington Gap was not going to happen. Star General was one of the many hospitals in the region that took it upon themselves to run background checks on their patients and alert the authorities if anyone had outstanding warrants. Cunningham had been on the lam for the last 15 months for obstructing justice and violating probation. So, he needed to get to Washington Cove in Coeburn, and fast, but as his health declined, a weakness was ebbing in on him, and he knew that he couldn't make that drive himself. So, he was driving home to get his wife.

Cunningham was certain that he had several broken ribs, a fractured eye socket, and flusters of contusions around every corner of his body. He escaped the crash but not the scowl of that goddamn Sheriff Dougherty, who was slowly driving past as Cunningham made a run for it. What the hell was he doing in Pennington Gap? Cunningham didn't hang around to ask him. Freah and Merle were either dead or unconscious—there was no time for him to make certain of anything because an accident of that degree surely alerted the law and surrounding people.

Minutes later, Cunningham turned onto his street, and as he drew near, he saw someone in his driveway. Instinctively, he reached for his gun in the passenger seat, but upon narrowing his eyes, he saw that it was Ginger—she was putting a suitcase inside the trunk of her car. He sped into the driveway to block her in. The glower of the headlights heightened her look of terror.

Getting out of the car, Cunningham grabbed his side as a burst of excruciating pain shot through the left region of his torso. Ginger noticed.

"And where the hell do you think you're going?" he grumbled.

Ginger backed away cautiously, her heart pounding in her chest. The weight of her decision felt like a thousand pounds pressing down on her, but it had been building for so long, she couldn't ignore it anymore. Every argument, every slap, every broken promise—it had chipped away at the love she once had for him, until there was nothing left but this suffocating fear.

This is it, Ginger thought. This is the end of it all. I can't keep living like this. I deserve more than this. My son deserves more than this.

She could feel the tears welling up in her eyes, but she wiped them away quickly, angry at herself for being weak. She had to be strong now. For herself. For her son.

"I can't do this anymore."

Her voice cracked with the weight of the words. The decision had been made, but it still felt like a betrayal—like she was abandoning him. She felt his eyes burning into her, but she couldn't look back. Not now. The thought of leaving, of walking away from everything she knew, made her stomach twist. *What if he comes after me? What if I'm making the biggest mistake of my life? But I can't stay here . . . not like this. Not with him hurting me, hurting our son.*

Cunningham peered inside her car and saw his son strapped securely in his car seat. He had caught her in the act of leaving him.

The demand, the threat in his voice, was enough to freeze her. She turned to face him, fighting back the fear and the guilt gnawing at her.

"Get in the house, now!"

"No. I mean it. I'm done."

The finality of her words hung in the air between them like a thick fog. Her knees almost buckled from the weight of her emotions. She could hear her son's soft whimpers from inside the car, and it broke her heart, but she had to stay strong.

He'll be okay. He'll understand one day.

Cunningham's expression twisted in anger, and before she could react, he was on her, his hand around her throat. The shock of his touch made her vision blur with panic, but it wasn't the physical pain that hurt the most—it was the betrayal in his eyes, the complete disregard for her humanity.

In a blur of desperation, she fought back, punching, kicking, screaming for help as the neighbors started to stir. Every part of her body screamed to break free, but her strength was fading. *Why can't he just let me go? Why does he have to do this?*

She felt her energy drain with every blow, her resolve slipping away. *Why did I ever think I could fix this?*

When he headbutted her, the world went dark for a moment. Her body went limp in his grasp, and the pain that followed was all-consuming, but there was also a strange feeling of relief. *It's over. It's finally over.*

"Bitch," he growled, and the words hit her like a physical blow, but she didn't care anymore. Her eyes closed as her body sagged in his grip. She had made her choice.

. . . "Take us home, baby," Ginger pleaded. "We wanna go home."

"Stop lying. You were gonna take my son away from me, bitch."

"Don't do this, please. We're—"

"You did this!"

Cunningham raked his fingers through his oily black hair, then stormed off, screaming at the top of his lungs. His life was crap, and it was just getting shittier by the minute. His addiction was getting the better of him—sleep deprivation had him delusional and seeing doubles. Plus, the loss of blood didn't help any.

He texted Teddy Lee, then hurled his phone into a tree, shattering the device. He was tired of having the weight of the world on his shoulders. An inglorious bastard who failed to amount to anything memorable. A loser who was tired of losing.

He took a deep breath, then turned on the heels of his boots and walked back to the car, saying loud enough for Ginger to hear, "You wanna go home? I'll take you home."

Climbing behind the steering wheel, Cunningham gunned the accelerator, and the rear tires spun in place before taking off. Cunningham weaved between the trees recklessly. The car bumbled up and down on the uneven terrain. Tears streamed down his face—he loved Ginger to death—literally. The car sped beyond the edge of the grove and toward the pier of Lake Chahoogee.

Spliiiish!

As the car sank beneath the depths of the ice-cold water, Ginger's heart raced, her breath coming in short, panicked gasps. The freezing water rushed in, and she screamed, her voice drowned out by the deafening roar of the sinking car. Her mind was spinning, the terror consuming her. This can't be happening. I can't die like this... Her hands fumbled helplessly at the door handle, but it was no use. The water kept rising, cold and unforgiving.

Beside her, her son wailed in terror, his tiny hands pounding the seat, as if he could somehow fight off the inevitable. Ginger grabbed him, pulling him close, feeling the frantic pulse of his tiny heart against her chest. Please, please, God, help us, she thought, but the words felt empty. The pressure of the water increased, and she could feel it crushing down on her chest, making it harder to breathe. She kissed her son's forehead, her tears mixing with the cold water. She whispered, her voice shaking with fear, "I love you, baby. I love you."

Through the terror and panic, she caught a glimpse of Cunningham beside her—his face eerily calm as the water filled his lungs and stomach. He had made peace with it. But

I won’t, not like this, she thought. She wasn’t ready to die. Not like this. Not with her son.

She screamed again, her voice cracking with the finality of it all. The water was up to her neck now, and she could feel her strength leaving her, her body growing numb. She held onto her son for dear life, praying that somehow, some way, they would make it out. But as the cold closed in, her thoughts faded into the murky darkness.

***

Meanwhile . . .

Savannah walked out the door of her house with the straps of an overnight bag slung over her shoulder. Her husband was awaiting her. It was time to finish this. Her phone rang, and she stopped to reach into her back pocket for it. It was a group video chat from Freah and Lisette.

“Hey,” she answered.

“Have y’all left yet?” Freah asked.

“No,” Savannah told her.

“Okay. Well, me and Becka are already here,” Lisette said. “Ready as ever.”

“And Squirrel and us are leaving now,” Freah added with a faint smile. “He said not to forget his dynamite and—”

Savannah cut her off, directing the camera lens of her phone to her overnight bag. “I got everything.”

The three sister-in-laws spoke for a few more seconds, then Savannah ended the call. If Teddy Lee thought the White Boys were a problem, wait until he got a load of them White Girls. They were worse.

Chapter 20

Errol and Harley climbed into the truck. Words escaped them. This was an unusual predicament, one that neither of them had an immediate solution for.

Vehicles pulled in and out of the parking lot of the hospital. They watched. A horn blared. There was some bass. Doors slammed. They listened.

Errol turned the key in the ignition to heat the cab, because although they were both overwhelmed by a numbing sensation of pain, the bitter cold was biting like hell.

It's not her fault, it's not her fault, it's not her fault, Errol continuously told himself.

It's not my fault, it's not my fault, it's not my fault, Harley continuously told herself.

They looked at each other, then broke eye contact. They were both uncomfortable. They had wanted this connection for so long, and now that they had it, the universe was attempting to rip it apart.

I can't let them kill my pa', Harley told herself.

They looked at one another questioningly, wondering what the other was possibly thinking. Harley took hold of his hand. Her touch melted the ice that was forming around his heart.

"What are we gonna do?" she asked him.

He sighed. "Hell if I know."

Harley's eyes saddened. Was this the end of a beautiful start?

"I don't want to lose you, Errol. This time with you has been the best moments of my life, and I don't want it to end."

Her words moved him. "Ever?" he said.

"Ever, baby."

Errol understood the meaning . . . forever was exactly what he desired, as well. He was a sucker for love at heart. When he was a boy, he used to look forward to hearing his parents tell him how they met and how trying it was—two lost teenagers who found themselves through each other. They protected their relationship from envious outsiders who wanted what they had—they worked every day at creating a world of their own.

"A broken bone is easier to mend than a broken heart, son," his mother once told him. "So don't be so fast to break your own over the wrong one, because you may not recover."

"I like the sound of that," he said to Harley. "Has a nice ring to it. Ever," he let the word roll off his tongue.

This was bad. These mixed emotions were driving these two insane. Their eyes drifted back to the windshield, panning the uneven fuel parking lot. These young bucks had killed for one another. There was no running back now. Or was there? And if there was a game being played, which one of the two was playing it?

A vehicle turned into the parking lot and rode past the truck. Errol immediately recognized its occupants—Billy and Squirrel. The car pulled to a stop at the entrance doors, and a minute later, Freah and Robin walked out of the hospital.

Errol reached for his door handle, saying to Harley, "I'll be back."

"What? What are you gonna do?"

He looked at her. "I don't know, but I gotta try something."

Harley watched Errol run between parked vehicles while flagging his hand in the air, yelling for his mother.

Harley crawled over the console and into the passenger seat.

"Errol, what did I tell you?" Freah said.

"Mom, listen. I—"

Scuurr!

Tires peeled, drawing the attention of everyone within earshot.

"Harley!" Errol yelled, running to catch up to his truck.

But she was gone.

Chapter 21

Four Harley-Davidson motorcycles pulled into the yard of the house, and seconds later, Jim Bob and Starks walked out the front door to greet their fellow Infidels—Turbo, Bruiser, Ray, and Nick.

"Tell me it's some cold beer in there?" Bruiser said, removing his helmet.

Jim Bob smiled. "Shit, son, a fridge without beer is a useless one, by George."

"Where's Teddy?" Nick asked, dismounting. "I don't see his bike."

"Inside. Got Candy here," Starks answered with a grin.

Candy was the biggest biker whore in Lee County—pussy so good it was rumored to make men leave their wives, jobs, and entire identity behind.

Ray chuckled. "Boy must gotta lotta shit on his mind to have her over here."

"Yeah, 'cause last time I was with her, I couldn't remember my goddamn name or what state I was from."

They shared a humorous moment about how Candy Phillips would make one forget all about their problems.

Jim Bob led the boys into the house. Dog Man and Jaxon were sitting at the kitchen table playing Tonk, and each of the bikers swatted Dog Man on the back of his head as they bypassed the table on their way to the living room. Jaxon lowered his head angrily—he hated the Infidels.

Dog Man took several deep breaths; his patience was running thin, but he had to remind himself of the level of violence these shitheads were capable of. He thought back to that cold morning on High Knob Mountain . . .

. . . Dog Man spit in Teddy Lee's face, then snapped, saying, "Do what you will, you cock-bleeding sumbitch. But I promise you, my brother's gone—"

Teddy Lee swung his mighty hammer into Dog Man's ribcage, and a sickening crack sounded. Dog Man's mouth popped wide, and a guttural gasp escaped his throat.

"Tell Satan I sent you, boy," Teddy Lee said through clenched teeth. "I know 'em, personally." He swung his hammer again.

"No, wait, please," Dog Man managed to say in a strained tone of voice. "I . . . haven't . . ." he struggled to breathe properly. "Haven't backed out."

"That's exactly what you've done, boy. You came to me for help, now you and that nappy-headed son of yours are out to get that goddamn mixture for yourselves, by God."

Dog Man feigned a look of confusion, a gesture that indicated that he didn't have a clue about the button-sized listening devices that Teddy Lee had planted in certain places—his leather jacket that he was currently wearing, and in his truck. Teddy Lee listened to the entire conversation that Dog Man had with Merle this morning—it's how Teddy Lee pinpointed his whereabouts to ambush him and Gene, but little did Teddy Lee know—he was the one who was in the dark.

"Didn't think I knew about that, did you?" Teddy Lee said smugly, feeling quite proud of himself. "I got eyes on ya', boy."

"Oh, goddamn, goddamn," Gene cried. "Goddamn."

Dog Man and Gene were bound to the tree by thick, lumbering rope that Jim Bob and Cunningham wrapped around their torsos, taped off with a fisherman's knot. The rope worked as a layered shield that minimized the impact of the sledgehammer to the extent of saving his life—it would've damaged a lot more than a couple of ribs.

"Goddamn, goddamn."

Gene had taken just as much of a beating as Dog Man.

"I can get Merle to cough it up, I swear," Dog Man said. "Fake . . . Fake my death," he swallowed and drew a guttural breath that resembled fluid in the lungs. "Gives me room to sneak 'round a bit," another ragged breath. "Get what we both want. They'll be looking for y'all to attack, but I'll be in the shadows . . . dead."

Teddy Lee arched a brow questioningly. "Fake your death? How do you intend to get away with that?"

Dog Man looked to his left at Gene and said, "Put my credentials on 'em and bash his goddamn face in."

Gene couldn't believe what Dog Man just suggested. "Oh, goddamn, goddamn, goddamn," he said nervously.

"He's the Sheriff's brother and his personal little snitch."

"Snitch?" Cunningham said with a mug. "Hell yo' mean, boy?"

"I mean he's telling. Set up a few of my guys down in Inkly Bottom."

Jim Bob narrowed his eyes suspiciously and said, "Then why in Sam hell are you with 'em?"

A sharp jolt of pain caused Dog Man to wince. "I . . . I was gonna take 'em out to pasture and put 'em down."

Teddy Lee looked to his boys for their opinion.

"Reckon it'll work," said Jim Bob.

"Maybe it won't," Cunningham countered. "I say we kill these jiggaboos and take it to Merle head-on. He'll give us that damn recipe, by God."

"If you believe that, then you don't know Merle," Dog Man said.

Teddy Lee had to agree. "Sumbitch'll die before he gives it up."

"Merle is all about family. We gotta take what he values the most to break him. And like I said, they're waiting for you boys, y'all's intention is widely known. Let me do this."

Teddy Lee weighed his options. He heard the heated exchange between Merle and Dog Man this morning. Merle was adamant about his purpose and reason for not agreeing to Dog Man's proposal. He sized the two captives up. Gene and Dog Man shared two similarities—their height and mocha-colored skin complexion.

Without a second thought, Teddy Lee raised his sledgehammer high above his head.

Dog Man closed his eyes and murmured a quick prayer.

"Oh, goddamn, goddamn, god—"

Teddy Lee drove that hammer dead smack into Gene's face. Thwack!

Dog Man shouted frighteningly—feeling the splatter of bone and blood as Teddy Lee continuously beat Gene's head to mush . . .

… Dog Man shook the memory loose and laid a 2-3-4 spread onto the table. "Tonk," he said to Jaxon.

"Where's that nigger's brother?" Dog Man heard Turbo say from the living room.

"Sumbitch in the closet," Jim Bob said. "We worked 'em over real good."

Bruiser chuckled. "Which should be the treatment of all niggers."

"Ha. Now you're talking tradition, pal," Ray said.

"Let's not hold those beers up."

***

Teddy Lee stood up from the bed to pull his jeans on. A single lamp on the floor illuminated the bedroom that consisted of only a bed and chair. Candy, naked as a jaybird, rolled to her side and lit a cigarette. Sex with Teddy Lee was incredible—he touched regions far inside the tulip that no man has ever reached.

Teddy Lee reached to the floor for his phone and saw that not only did he have several missed calls, but also a text message from Cunningham. He opened the message.

Cunningham: She tried to leave me, bro. Just as everyone else have. I'm tired, Friend. Good luck. I'm going home to momma.

Teddy Lee closed his eyes to combat his tears. Suicide was a topic that was frequently ignored in his outfit, but many of his boys suffered from mental illness—Cunningham being one of them. Darkness was the ground rules of every outlaw. They have seen and done too much to maintain the reins of normalcy—it's days that one don't want to get up . . . feeling trapped, helpless. Teddy Lee personally understood the psychosis of unrelenting emotions and pain. A "Death- gotta-be-easier-'cause-life-is-hard" kind of thing.

"Damn, brother," he murmured.

Candy caressed his back. "You say something, sweety?" she asked him.

"No," he said, wiping his eyes.

Teddy Lee and Cunningham had been friends since they were boys, and his loyalty to him and the Infidels was an undying commitment that Teddy Lee had come to love and appreciate.

He called Cunningham's phone—straight to voicemail. He called again . . . same. A part of him didn't want to believe that his second-in-command was really dead. He called again, and just when he thought to call one of his men to spin up through Pennington Gap to check on his friend, an incoming call interrupted that notion—it was Harley.

His face turned beet red. With everything that had transpired between him and Bobbi Dupree, Teddy Lee had tried his hardest to disown the fact that Harley was indeed his flesh and blood—especially after gathering sight of Holly—even more so after that point, but Harley was a replica of his mother, so much that he couldn't deny his footprints in the sands of time—18 years of jumbled emotions and resentment have hindered his love and devotion for his only child.

But Teddy Lee had always been an irrationally impulsive man, so as much as the voice inside his head instructed him to not jump to conclusions and talk to his daughter sensibly, warmly, sincerely, instead he answered her call with a sneer.

"You low-down, nigger-loving bitch!"

"Don't you take that goddamn tone with me, you sumbitch," Harley fired back. "I don't owe you a goddamn thang, hear? Now—"

Teddy Lee stood up from the bed, his body as rigid as a room full of Republicans.

"You bets take it down a notch, hear. I don't—"

She cut him off. "I love 'em."

He stomped his foot and shouted, "You don't know shit about love. Especially to some goddamn porch monkey."

"Shut up, shut up!" she shouted. "You don't even fucking know 'em. Don't call 'em that."

A tear fell from Teddy Lee's eye. She was obviously far too gone—her choice of words conveyed as much.

"Pa', where are you? The Whites are—"

"Fuck the Whites. I'm-ma—"

"This ain't a fucking game, Pa'. They're coming for you."

"Then let 'em come, goddammit!"

Harley began to cry. "No."

Teddy Lee lowered his head. She was trying to protect him. The sound of her tears crushed his heart to dust.

"Harley, stay out of this," he said.

"How?" she asked.

He ended the call.

Chapter 22

While holding tightly on to the handle of his gun, Dougherty walked Merle to the house with a watchful eye.

"You Whites really thank y'all shit don't stank, but by God you summabitches stank to high heaven, I tell ya'. Running around here like y'all royalty or something, ruining our beautiful little town with that poison of y'all's. I'm sick of it," he said.

"I don't know what the hell you're talking about," was all that Merle had to say. He wasn't a man who openly admitted or spoke about things that could incriminate him—conditioned to deflect even under such circumstances as this.

"You know damn well what I'm talking about. Damn mess of y'all's got my damn brother killed," Dougherty snapped.

Merle looked at him strangely.

"That sidewinder brother of yours put you dumb sumbitches in the trick bag, but I caught on to 'em, by George. Dog Man ain't dead yet," Dougherty added.

Merle's perplexed expression deepened. "Say again?" he asked.

Dougherty didn't like to repeat himself. "You heard me just fine, boy," he said.

They ascended the steps of the porch. Dougherty directed Merle to a chair while keeping a trained eye on the front door.

"Where's Lisette?" he asked Merle.

"Bristol," Merle answered.

"Oh yeah. And what's in Bristol?"

"People," Merle replied.

Dougherty smacked him in his face with his gun. "Don't get smart with me, boy," he snarled.

Merle spat a glob of blood onto Dougherty's boots. "And the Corner Dog House," he said with a chuckle. "Best goddamn sandwich ever."

"Yeah, keep laughing, asshole," Dougherty said, reaching inside his pocket for his phone. "I might just dump your body behind that place."

Merle's bloody grin evaporated. This was no laughing matter.

After a minute of tapping on the screen of his phone, Dougherty turned the device around to show Merle the video of Rock-on's abduction.

"Rock-on's been taken. By Dog Man and Jaxon, no less," Dougherty stated.

Merle watched the footage in utter disbelief. Dougherty could see both pain and confusion etched in Merle's features.

"He owes me his life," Dougherty said once the video ended. "And I intend to be paid in full."

In all seriousness, Merle told him, "You're gonna get everything that you got coming to you."

"You're damn right I am," Dougherty replied.

Dougherty kicked the front door in, then quickly upped his pistol, but nothing happened—not a sound, but his hair was still standing on end. The thought of Squirrel barging out of the house put his teeth on edge.

"Get up," he ordered Merle. "Walk." He pushed Merle on his back.

Merle, hands bound to his rear, nearly tripped over the threshold, saying, "Take it easy, bub."

Dougherty flipped a light switch and the shadowy figures of the sunken living room came to life—wooden lacework and seductive, low-slung suede sofas. Dougherty scanned the room, the gas-burning wall sconces, ivory art sculptures, and burnished walnut railing of the central staircase.

"Whole town going to shit, and y'all rotten scoundrels living high off the hog," he said with a tinge of jealousy in his voice.

Merle didn't comment.

"But the streets are like chasing tornadoes. It's thrilling until you're caught in the eye of that motherfucker." Dougherty clocked him good in the back of his head with the butt of his gun. Merle crumpled to the floor unconscious. "I'm that eye."

Dougherty removed the zip tie from Merle's wrists, dragged his body to an upright position, and leaned him against a closet door, whereupon after retrieving a pair of handcuffs from his back pocket, he slapped a cuff around his wrist, then clasped the second bracelet around the doorknob.

"You finally done put too much dip on your chip, boy," Dougherty said to Merle, then stepped off to search the house. He needed some answers.

Merle opened his eyes and watched Dougherty ascend the stairs with his gun extended. *The sheriff will die here tonight—along with the others.*

"Fuck the police," Merle murmured.

And at that moment the gates of hell opened and the most triumphant classical rock instrumental played as the following events unraveled in slow motion . . .

***

Highway 10 was a lonely stretch of cedar trees and litter.

The full moon hung above, its craters glowing softly in the sky, casting a pale light as three vehicles sped down the highway.

Car # 1. Rock-on was behind the wheel, and he and Savannah shared a joint, the smoke curling up into the cool night air..

Car # 2. Lisette drove with a cigarette between her lips and a can of beer between her thighs. Seated in the passenger seat was Dog Man's and Lisette's older daughter, Becka, carefully loading the clip of a M-16, her focus sharp.

Car # 3. Billy was driving the SUV. Errol, from the back seat, watched his mother, Squirrel, and Robin load bullets into magazines. His thoughts drifted to Harley, and a sadness washed over him. He missed her.

Up ahead, huge green sign read: *Welcome to Lee County*. A deer, scavenging for food, discovered a discarded Burger King bag that had a half-eaten burger inside it, but before it could indulge in its finding, the three speeding vehicles passed by, and scared the dickens out of the poor creature.

The Whites had arrived.

The Hitters ...

***

Dog Man was shuffling the deck of cards when he felt his phone vibrate inside his pocket. Before reaching to retrieve his device, he looked toward the living room to make certain that no one was watching him—he was in the clear.

It was a text message from his wife

Lisette: *We're here, babe*.

Dog Man slipped his phone back into his pocket, then looked at Jaxon and gave him a nod of confirmation.

The Insiders...

***

Teddy Lee stood by the bedroom window, his hands gripping an AK-47 assault rifle as he peered out through the blinds.

Candy lay in bed, propped on her elbow, her face marked by worry.

Teddy Lee turned to her, and said: "Get dressed. You got ta go."

And with that said, he exited the bedroom shirtless. There was something off about him—a look of fierce determination, but . . . buggy . . . insane.

The Underdog . . .

***

Harley paced within the high beams of the truck, her phone pressed to her ear. The whites of her eyes were red, and she just didn't look herself.

She looked at the screen of her phone—her father's name and number. He wasn't answering.

Frustrated, Harley stamped her foot and screamed to the heavens, her voice raw with emotion.

***

The Torn . . .

Merle slipped his finger inside the tiny pocket that was within the larger pocket of his pants, retrieving a hidden handcuff key. There was one thing that Sheriff Dougherty was going to learn about Merle White tonight—he played chess, not checkers.

Merle then took a high-powered crossbow with steel-tipped bolts from the closet and, moving quietly, crept up the steps.

The Mastermind . . .

***

Dougherty entered the master bedroom and flicked the light switch on, but immediately flipped it back off. What was that? He crossed the floor to the far wall while staring at a thin strip of light along the baseboard. Lowering himself to his knees, Dougherty peered into the crack and saw table legs and small wheels, like those of office chairs. The air was cool, filled with the scent of potpourri.

Dougherty's hands ran over the wall—it was hard as steel. Pressing against it, the wall slid upward with little noise, like a window opening.

Dougherty couldn't believe his eyes. It was a secret lair. He slowly entered the brightly lit room that greatly resembled the law office of any detective unit across the country. As he moved closer, he saw a wall lined with photos—his mouth dropped open at the sight of the confidential informants working on *Operation White Wash*, the investigation into the Whites and their affiliates. His brother's photograph was marked with a red "X" across his face.

There were also pictures of Teddy Lee and his crew—an ongoing investigation into targets they'd been tracking. But then, Dougherty's eyes froze on one photo in particular. It was of himself, sitting at an outdoor café with his wife, Edna, in downtown Norton.

His hand reached up to tear the photo down, but before he could, an arrow shot through his palm, pinning it to the wall with a sickening thud.

"Ahhh!" Dougherty cried.

The Dead Man…

***

Big Dennis Emery cried out painfully and fell against the refrigerator door as blood skeeted on the linoleum floor and down onto his sock and house slipper . . . warm—thick.

Squirrel twisted the eight-inch blade of his KA-BAR knife, then yanked it free of Emery's calf.

"Fuuuck!" Emery cursed.

"That's exactly what you are," Freah said before plugging two hollow-point bullets into the back of his head.

Big Dennis Emery was an enforcer for the White Infidels—WAS! Now he only serves purpose to the maggots.

***

Dog Man closed the refrigerator door and walked back to the table with two beers in his hand. Sliding one to Jaxon, he twisted the lid of his own and took a sizable gulp, but abruptly lowered the bottle from his lips upon seeing Teddy Lee enter the living room with an AK-47 in his hand. Everyone looked at him strangely.

"What's up, boss?" Jim Bob asked.

Teddy Lee swung the closet door open and Swiss-cheesed Rock-on's body—or so they all thought was Rock-on.

They all looked at Teddy Lee with disbelief; he just killed their leverage, but he didn't offer an explanation. He just took a seat and reached to the coffee table for a meth pipe.

Seconds later, Candy came running out from the back of the house half-dressed en route to the front door.

Teddy Lee laid his head back on the sofa and released a thick stream of smoke—his eyes went glassy, a glaze of euphoria—just the trials of a gang . . .

***

Harley sped into the driveway of her father's house. The 1800s Colonial was dark, and it looked as though a week's worth of newspapers littered the yard. She hopped down from the cab and ran for the door.

"Pa'," she yelled while knocking firmly. "Pa', it's Harley."

She ran around the side of the house to the back.

***

Dougherty swung his body right to take aim at his assailant, but he was caught by his wrist by a strong meaty hand—Merle.

Merle headbutted him, then snatched the arrow from his wound.

***

T.J. Bausch lost control of the car, causing it to flip several times before landing on its roof in the lot of an abandoned Revco drugstore. Flames erupted from the undercarriage, leaving no time to spare.

Bausch, bleeding from multiple gunshot wounds, struggled to crawl out the driver-side window, the shattered glass cutting into his skin as he tried to escape.

Rock-on pulled to a stop—just mere feet from the wreckage—and Savannah hopped out the car to finish the bastard off.

"Wrong family, fucker," she told Bausch, then racked her shotgun and blew his fucking face off.

Savannah White was the true definition of a "blonde bombshell." T.J. Bausch was the Infidels' Head of Operations—now he didn't have a head at all.

Savannah got into the car and Rock-on peeled off.

***

Dog Man and Jaxon watched Turbo and Brusiere carry the body out the door of the house. They gave each other a look, then went back to playing their card game.

Teddy Lee eyed them menacingly from the living room sofa—taking a swig from a bottle of Jim Beam, his finger caressed the trigger of his AK-47. He was losing sight of himself.

***

Harley was driving through the narrow alleys of Skid Row—a poorly built, rundown part of Lee County that her father usually conducted business at. But tonight, all she saw were lingering addicts and stray dogs wandering aimlessly.

Her phone rang. It was Errol calling. She tapped the "Fuck you" button and sent him directly to voicemail. Her eyes welled up with tears—it pained her to hurt him.

***

Merle slapped the handcuffs around Dougherty's wrist, then pushed him on his chest—forcing him to take a seat, whereupon Merle immediately began punching his lights out.

***

Kevin Mowry grabbed his car keys from off of the coffee table and headed for the door—he had a hot piece of ass waiting for him on the other side of town, so he had to make way.

Upon opening the door, Lisette plunged a butcher knife into his abdomen with tremendous force, and Kevin heard a "pop," then the god-awful stench of his inner intestines raced up through his nostrils. A yelp escaped him, and the ring of keys fell from his grasp and landed on the floor with a jingle.

With a hateful snarl, Lisette ran him against a wall by the handle of the knife. "Bastard," she said. "Don't fuck with my fam—"

Kevin hooked her with a stiff right, and she staggered to a knee with a busted lip. He then pulled the knife from his wound and raised it above his head to drive the blade into Lisette's skull, but Becka appeared in the doorway and snagged his attention—she was clutching twin Berettas and didn't hesitate to release hell upon that son of a bitch.

Becka White. Mixed breed. Twenty-two years old and a total fucking badass.

Kevin Mowry was a high-ranking lieutenant in the Infidels—demoted to a low-level corpse.

Lisette wiped her mouth with the back of her hand, then kicked Kevin in his mouth. She was one country gal not to fuck with. Scooping her knife up from the floor, Lisette followed Becka out the door.

***

Dog Man was sitting on the lip of the bathtub loading bullets into the clip of his gun. Inserting the magazine, he put one in the head, then stood up to tuck the weapon securely in the waistline of his jeans.

Approaching the sink, Dog Man stared at his reflection in the mirror—there was this now-or-never look in his eyes.

***

Harley was parked roadside on her phone, scrolling through images of her and Errol.

"Kissy-faces." "Hugs at the river." "Georgie's party." "Dishes of food that they prepared together." "Humorous photos of their epic food fight."

Through her tears, she laughed.

***

Merle had knocked Dougherty unconscious. Several bones in the sheriff's face were either fractured or broken, leaving it swollen and bruised, a mess of puffed-up flesh.

Merle was standing at the wall of photographs—removing selective ones and dropping them in a trash bin.

Gene Dougherty.

Big Dennis Emery.

T. J. Bausch.

Kevin Mowry.

And others.

***

Freah, Squirrel, Billy, and Robin were all walking back to the SUV as an inferno roared in the background.

The house that once belonged to Henry McBeth, the Brand Ambassador for the Infidels, was now reduced to ashes. Henry and his wife, Marlee, had been left as nothing but charred remains.

Seated in the SUV, Errol stared at his family with an incredulous expression written on his face—he couldn't believe that they were capable of the violent acts he had seen them carry out tonight.

Chapter 23

Dougherty was awake at this point, and he was eyeing Merle who was removing a photograph of Henry Mcbeth from the wall. Dougherty knew of Henry. He was the Brand Ambassador for the Infidels, and by all accounts, a snappy little son of a bitch.

"You wanted me to find this room, didn't you?" Dougherty asked him, his voice hoarse.

Merle looked at him with a small grin. "That I did, James. Because out of all the people on this wall, I hate our rotten ass the most. And that speaks volumes, considering that a number of these motherfuckers are rats, and the others wanna kill me and my family."

Merle lit a cigarette, inhaling deeply before turning back to the wall. "Teddy Lee's a man who's driven off pain."

"And you know that, how?" Dougherty replied, raising an eyebrow.

"An act of betrayal is what paved his path. We were friends. Which was something that his family was totally against. Racism runs deep in his family." Merle paused thoughtfully. "But he didn't care what they thought or felt," Merle looked at Dougherty. "He was just a great guy."

Dougherty scoffed. "So great, he tryna kill ya'."

"A scorned man is an unpredictable nightmare, James," Merle shot back, his voice cool. "Slight a devil and expect a demon."

"And the devil being?"

Merle's gaze lingered on Teddy Lee's photo. "Disloyalty."

There was a moment of silence.

"As you know, I have a big family, James," Merle continued, his voice steady but intense. "And sure, they all have their own thangs going on, or whatnot, but there's something that I've come to learn."

"Which is?" Dougherty asked, his voice laced with curiosity.

Merle eased down into a chair, his tone smoothy but heavy with meaning as he said: "It's always been my story. I've created structure, a means, a way to escape the goddamn hole that your so-called god tossed us in." His eyes darkened, his jaw tightening. "And now you're trying to push us back down in there. A place that you don't know shit—"

Dougherty shouted. "Don't tell me what the fuck I know, Merle. I had to watch my family drown on the fucked-up piece of land that your pa' sold us."

Merle's eyes flashed. "He didn't—"

"Maybe he did know," Dougherty snapped, his anger simmering. "Saw that it was soft in spots and knew one day that it'll all sink."

Merle waved his hand dismissively. "Land give way everywhere, James, all over, you sumbitch, and if ya' speak sideways 'bout my pa' again, Imma smack yo' black ass silly.

Silence hung in the air.

Merle leaned back, his voice lowering but full of resolve. "Like I told you, it's my story, and in my story my family walks off into the sunset, and the rest of you die."

Dougherty shook his head, a bitter laugh escaping his lips. "Your story sucks," he said sarcastically.

Merle's gaze curled into a smirk. "At the point of you putting rats in the swang of thangs, yes."

Dougherty's gaze shifted to the wall, his eyes scanning the images pinned across it— each informant he had assigned to '*Operation Whiteout*' was amongst the extensive collage of classified intel.

"You have someone on the inside?" Dougherty said

Merle took a slow drag from his cigarette. "I'll be a fool not to." . . .

… Patrick knocked on Maddy Smith's door. She was the Data Technician, and a mighty damn good one, but he has never cared much for the pompous woman. Her self-importance was off the charts—she either considered herself the smartest person in the room or gods' gift to men, neither of which were true.

"Enter," came her high-pitched voice.

"Hey. You busy?" Patrick asked her, stepping inside.

Maddy swiveled her chair away from her impressive display of screens and gizmos, giving him a condescending look. "Unlike a lot of you, I actually show up to work, Patrick." She flashed a phony smile and rolled her eyes. "What do you want?"

Patrick closed the door behind him. "Is the system back up?"

"Yes."

"Pop wants you to retrace the tracks of this phone." He gave her Freah's device. "It's unlocked."

Maddy's features lightened, which did nothing to heighten her gothic-like appearance. "Great," She said drily, her voice flat . . .

. . . "Maddy?" Dougherty asked, a disbelieving look crossing his face.

"She's a wonder, by George," Merle replied with a smirk. "I watched her hack your computer from her phone. I'll make sure she's the next sheriff of Norton." He grinned. "It'll be my department then, won't it?"

This pissed Dougherty off. "No matter what you do to me, you won't get away with this, you bastard. Patrick—"

Merle cut him off with a smirk. “Is here.”

Dougherty's forehead creased in confusion. “What?”

“He’s here. So’s your wife and the rest of your kids.” Merle jerked his head toward a door at the far end of the room.

“I’ll kill you!” Dougherty yelled, lunging from his chair to headbutt Merle in the face.

Merle caught him by the throat with one hand and slapped him with the other. He backhanded him, then smacked him again, backhanded him once more, before spitting in his face. With a grunt, he slung Dougherty to the floor.

“Don’t threaten me with a good time, motherfucker,” Merle said coldly, kicking him in the ribs. “Now,” he kicked him again, “get,”*—another kick—*“your ass up,”*—another kick—*“in that chair.”

A minute passed. Dougherty struggled to pull himself together. The two former schoolmates glared at each other, their expressions full of venom.

“You envy what I have, but my results came the hard way, son,” Merle said, his voice steady.

Dougherty sneered. “Reckon that helps you sleep better at night, huh?”

“That’s just it, James. No matter what I do, or who I do it to, sleep comes easy, boy.”

Dougherty’s eyes narrowed. He saw it . . . a fleeting glimpse of the goddamn devil.

“Merle, listen,” he said, his voice pleading. “I won’t say nothing, man. I’ll resign and leave town. Please, don’t do this.”

“You gave me no choice, James. When someone sets out to harm a man’s family, well, by George, that someone’s likely to catch the bull by the horns, son.”

Dougherty started tapping his foot nervously. “I can help Squirrel. Help him beat those charges, Merle, I swear I can.”

Merle reached for the handle of a desk drawer. “Is that right?”

"Darn tootin'. I'll get 'em thrown right out. He ain't gotta keep running like he is."

Merle pulled a plastic evidence bag from the drawer and laid it on the desk. Inside was Squirrel's gun—the murder weapon.

"Me and Maddy are working on making sure my brother's alright. But for right now, a little running don't hurt nobody."

Dougherty was sweating now, his eyes locked on the gun. He'd bagged and tagged it himself, so he knew its markings. If Maddy managed to swipe every piece of evidence from that murder scene, it would be grounds for dismissal—no witnesses, no evidence—and Squirrel would surely walk.

"Haven't enough people already gotten hurt, Merle? Davie. Savannah. Rock-on. It has to stop somewhere."

"Davie and Squirrel weren't supposed to go to Inkly Bottom," Merle shrugged, his tone casual. "But it happened, and we'll deal with it as a family."

"You're not gonna have any family after this. This thing you and Teddy Lee—"

"Over," Merle cut him off sharply.

Dougherty arched a brow in confusion.

"Savannah and Rock-on are helping wrap things up, as we speak."

"Wrap things up?" Dougherty echoed, obviously puzzled. "Hell you talkin' about?"

"I caught wind of Teddy Lee's intentions before he was even released from prison, son," Merle said, narrowing his eyes in all seriousness. "Do you think for one minute I was gonna let that yellow jack stang me? Kill my family and thangs?" He jabbed his finger into his chin repeatedly. "Not this hombre, son. Merle'll stand up in ya' chest about him, by George." He took a deep breath, trying to calm himself. Talking about his enemies always got him worked up. "So, I figured I'd kill two birds with one stone." He turned to the wall of images. "Rid my empire of the rats you sicked on us, while making Teddy Lee feel like he's gaining on me, when he's actually revealing the layout and players of his organization to none other . . ." He paused for dramatic effect. "Dog Man and Jaxon," he finished, pulling a photograph off the wall. It was of a bony-faced woman with bleached hair. "But with the sheriff's department holed up against us and Teddy Lee's listening devices set in place, we had to play our roles as if someone might be eavesdropping at all times."

"But we weren't," Dougherty offered, hoping to gain some leverage by revealing that he wasn't completely hell-bent on taking down the White family.

Merle shrugged. "No point in chancin' anything that could cost you your life."

"Says the drug dealer."

"That saved my life. There's a difference."

"How so, boy? It's the reason for all this."

"No. Snakes and rats are the reason for all this," Merle shot back sharply. "They're the ones who brang a dealer's life to ruin. Without them," he dropped the photograph onto Dougherty's lap, "the law ain't got no way in."

Dougherty looked at the picture, his voice dropping to a low murmur. "Jessica."

Jessica Laney; extreme meth addict and two-time loser who, after her third consecutive meth charge, signed on as a confidential informant to save her own skin.

"What you do to her, you sonofabitch?"

Merle grinned, the look on his face cold as ice. "Made her Savannah." . . .

. . . The storm had slowed to a drizzle, but Savannah didn't give a damn 'bout turning down the wipers or trimming the high beams. Her exit was comin' up, and all she could think 'bout was where she was headed.

She didn't bother to signal, either. Her Toyota Camry shot up the exit ramp, the tires makin' that wet, sloshing sound on the road beneath. When she stopped at a red light, she glanced into the sideview mirror. There had been a set of headlights on her tail ever since she left the house—Dog Man and Jaxon. She then flicked her eyes to the rearview to check on Jessica Laney, who they'd just put a beatdown on to make sure she was knocked out cold. They needed Jessica unrecognizable for this to work.

"Snitch-ass bitch," Savannah muttered under her breath. Even though Merle had swept her car for bugs, they couldn't be too sure of nothin' right now. "This your last ride."

The light turned green, and Savannah took a sharp left. Dog Man did the same. She glanced out the passenger side at an open field, all chopped up by deforestation, their entry point to the Gladdison Motel where Rock-on was waitin'.

Savannah slammed the gas pedal to the floor, jerking the wheel hard to the right. The Camry bounced onto the field, the car hoppin' in her seat with the rough ride.

Dog Man's truck tore onto the field with mad speed and rear-ended the Camry, slamming the truck lid open.

Savannah grabbed her gun before she yanked the door open, ready to leap out. The two cars tore across the muddy, slick field, fishtailin', flinging mud and chunks of straw everywhere . . .

. . . "She leapt out the car, leavin' Jessica to crash into the motel," Dougherty said, wrapping up the rest of the crazy mission. "Teddy Lee didn't know no better."

Merle nodded, his expression cool. "Apparently the dumb fuck only thought to bug Dog Man's truck and jacket," he shrugged. "His mistake, our gain."

Dougherty raised an eyebrow. "Why not just kill 'em? What's all this dog and pony shit?"

Merle gave him a look like he was straight-up stupid, then hit him with the reason. "And have his replacement comin' after me? Some half-cocked sumbitch who thinks he can't let me get away with killin' his boss?" He scoffed. "Only an idiot would think that doggone hunt's gonna work, son. Gangs only replace each other, so I'm leavin' nothin' to replace."

Merle shifted his focus to the wall, pulling off another photograph of one of Dougherty's informants. He laid it in Dougherty's lap on top of Jessica Laney's picture.

Dougherty glared down at it. It was Mary Anne Sawyer, a two-bit drug addict who'd been workin' for him for a minute.

"You put her on Rock-on," Merle said. "Like you did a few of 'em. And I get it—he's a party animal, the least focused of us all. But that boy got the instincts of a goddamn poker player, son. He can pick out liars and cheats in a heartbeat. He knew Mary Anne was a rat before Maddy even got her file."

Dougherty's jaw tightened. "What did you do to her?" His voice cracked a little, tryin' to hide his pain—he was havin' an affair with Mary Anne. "Tell me."

Merle didn't flinch. "She did it to herself, actually. We just laced the ice with some fentanyl, is all." . . .

. . . Rock-on watched his dick disappear into the dark depths of Mary Anne's wet asshole, thrusting fiercely, causing her cheeks to ripple like water. He held Mary Anne as she met his momentum, looking back at him with a *"Fuck me"* face, whilst the milk of her asshole splashed every which way.

"You fuck that shit. Fuck it," Mary Anne said, her tone aggressive but sultry at the same instance. "Goddamn that dick. Fuck yeah, fuck yeah."

Minutes later, a huge destructive disturbance jarred Rock-on from his state of ecstasy, and with Mary Anne tight on his heels, he hurried to the window to see what the hell was going on and saw that the front office of the motel was ablaze.

"What the hell?" he said, narrowing his eyes for a clearer view.

Rock-on sprinted back to the bed, throwin' on his clothes in a hurry, but not before he purposely left his wallet and an ounce of meth on the bedside table, like he was settin' it up for someone to find.

. . . "She stole some of the meth," Dougherty said, more of a statement than a question.

"Damn right, she did. Probably no damn sooner than my brother ran out of that room. Rats always take the cheese."

"She died?"

Merle nodded. "As all snitches should," he said, turning to the wall and saying from over his shoulder, "As you all will." He snatched a photo down.

Of course, Dougherty knew the man in the image. It was Jack Austin—Rock-on's best friend and Dougherty's star informant. Jack was snagged in a bust just a few months ago involving the solicitation of underage boys, in which Jack immediately stated that he could bring down the White Boys in exchange for complete exoneration of the stacked pedophilia charges.

"This is who you saw on the Burger Shack cameras," Merle said.

"I never said anything about no cameras."

"Didn't have to." . . .

. . . "I can stop this," Rock-on said quietly.

But there was only one problem. Only Dog Man and Merle knew the ingredients that boosted the quality of their Ice, but Dog Man was a hoarder, so somewhere in his house was that chemical recipe that will back the Infidels off from the family. Lisette and the kids were in Kingsport at Merle's warehouse, so the time to search their house was now.

Rock-on's phone chimed. It was a text message from Jaxon.

Jaxon: Jack just walked in. Front desk gave him the room number.

This was who they had been waiting for. Grabbing his coat from off of the back of the chair, Rock-on kissed Jessica Laney on her lips just in case Jack walked in, then he hurried out the door where he ran smack-dab into Jack.

"Whoa," said Jack. "Where you off to, bro'?"

"Jack," Rock-on said with faint surprise. "You came."

"Of course, you kidding? How is she?"

His expression saddened. "Not good. I was on my way to the house to get some of her things that I know she gone need when she wake up. I sure hate to leave her though, but—"

"Yeah, I get that. Hell, I can do it," Jack said.

"Yeah?"

"Yeah, but, ya' know, Winnie dropped me off, so I'mma need your car, and I'll call you when I get there so you can tell me what all to get," Jack added.

"I sure appreciate it. I just gotta get my laptop from out of the back seat," Rock-on said.

. . . "And from there Dog Man and Jaxon followed him."

. . . Merle nodded. "Teddy Lee has never met any of my brothers before, so it was easy to pass Jack off as Rock-on."

Dougherty lowered his gaze. Merle had pulled the wool over all of their eyes, and now here he was, a lawman wearing his own damn handcuffs.

"Do you really have my family behind that door, Merle?" he asked, looking him in his eyes.

"I do. And it's time you join 'em," Merle said.

Merle helped the sheriff stand up from his chair and escorted him to the door at the back of the room.

"You've always been a piece of shit to me, boy," Merle said. "But I ain't see no point to ruffle your feathers. But I tell ya, once I learned that you cut a pedophile a deal in exchange for us, I knew I'd be the one to make you regret that you were ever born, son," he said, using a key to unlock the door. "A real man would've put a bullet in that sumbitches head no sooner than the moon struck twelve."

"And how are you any different, Merle, huh? What about all the youngings 'round here strung out on your shit? Overdosing and robbing their own folks to fatten your pockets, huh? Far as I'm concerned, you're both scum," Dougherty countered.

Merle stared into his eyes. He was at a loss for words.

"Take me to my family," Dougherty told him, finally accepting his fate.

Merle opened the door, then moved aside to allow Dougherty to enter the last place that he will ever see—a cell block.

Dougherty's family, who were all locked inside separate cages, stood up from their bunks and ran to the doors of their steel confinements with hopeful expressions on their faces.

"Pa'!"

"James!"

"Daddy, what's going on?"

Merle forced Dougherty into a cage and locked the door without a hint of hesitation.

"The thought of me and my family rotting away in a cell made your dick hard, you bastard," Merle told Dougherty. "But this is me cutting your dick off."

"You can't leave us in here like this, you sonofabitch!" Dougherty said.

Merle's lips curled into a snarl. "Like hell I can't."

Merle turned around to take his leave. This was another closed chapter.

"Merle!"

Merle slammed the door shut behind him. He had heard enough of that bastard's voice.

"Fuck the police," he muttered.

Welcome To Death Row.

Chapter 24

Harley sped into the driveway of Holly's house and hopped out the truck without bothering to kill the engine. Holly was the last person that Harley ever thought she would need help from, but she didn't know who else to turn to. Running up the steps of the porch, a cat leapt out of a chair and up onto the banister—startling Harley. Holly loved cats and anything else that related to pussies and old folks. Holly was a wimp in every sense of the word. Harley had always been a pitbull gal, pythons, and fighting cocks. Twins, but they were as different as apples and oranges.

Harley tapped on the door, and seconds later, it swung open, and a funk smacked her in her face—filthy kitty litter and neglected hygiene. Harley stood eye to eye with her sister—same curvy frame and full pouty lips—but Holly was black, and to Holly, that was unpure and ugly.

"What the hell are you doing here?" Holly said with much attitude.

Harley pushed past her and kicked some junk aside before averting her eyes to the living room full of tweaking meth heads.

"Well, come on in," Holly said sarcastically.

"I see you're still following behind these losers," Harley said to Holly.

"Fuck you, you nigger-loving bitch," said Alex, Holly's 40-year-old boyfriend.

Harley grabbed a screwdriver from off the counter and charged into the living room. Alex leapt up from the couch and ran to a corner of the room, and just as Harley raised that Phillips head to impale that asswipe, Holly grabbed her by the arm.

"Harley, no!"

The other tweakers cleared out—they all knew who Harley's father was, but also they knew that she was just as crazy as he was.

Harley stared at her sister with wild eyes and flared nostrils.

"Please. He's all I got," Holly said.

This saddened Harley. Holly was so fucked up in the head that she truly believed that this racist piece of shit cared for her. And on top of that, who was she to Holly—chop suey?

Harley backed off, saying to Alex, "Try that again and I'll kill you, hear?" Alex nodded. "My sister's black, and that's just something you can't undo, you bastard, so watch that fucking word, inbred fuck. She's beautiful, and if y'all can't finally come to your fucking senses that color don't matter, you better get it 'cause I'm sick of it."

Holly stared at her sister admiringly. She had never heard Harley speak so defiantly in her defense before. Alex and others had called her 'nigger' so much that she was beginning to believe that it was her biological name. Lee County was short-handed on blacks, but this was her home, so she had always tried to make the best of it and fit in as much as possible.

"Now get somewhere safe while I talk to my sister, goddammit."

Alex quickly gathered his drug paraphernalia from off of the coffee table and hurried out of the room.

Harley dropped the screwdriver onto the seat of the recliner, then took a seat on the couch. Holly followed suit.

The sisters were born two minutes apart, but were not the ordinary set of twins by any means, and it wasn't until tonight that Harley completely understood how something like this could happen. Freah clarified a great deal of the mystery. Their mother had cheated on Teddy Lee with a man named Randy Shivers, who was from Norton, and from how Freah explained it, once a man ejaculates inside of a woman, it actually takes a full 24 hours for his seed to fertilize her reproductive organ, in which, at that particular interval, their mother had intercourse with another man, at which his semen became productive as well—the abnormal aftershock of a whore.

Holly had practically devoted her life to doing whatever she had to do to fit in with white folks. Whereas Harley had spent her life flowing against the grain. She would never forget the first black boy who snagged her heart. It was when their mother moved them to the housing projects in Bristol, Virginia. His name was Deangelo Brooks, and he was the most handsome boy that she had ever laid eyes on. They dated for a year, and throughout those months, Harley absorbed a great deal of black folks' culture, but she remained the country gal that they all came to love—then, out of the blue, her mother just up and moved them back to Lee County.

"What are you doing here?" Holly asked her.

Harley was direct. "Where are you scoring your dope from?"

Holly was thrown off by this. "What? Why? You don't—"

"I got a guy who's looking, is all. Ain't no need to be nosey."

Holly stared at her for a long minute. "Derick said you're dating a dealer, Harley. What gives?"

Harley reached to rid Holly's pretty green eye of a stray lash. "Derick's an ass. He's not a dealer, for Pete's sake."

Holly arched a brow. "He's a user, you mean?"

Harley stomped her foot irritably. "Holly!"

"Okay, sheesh. You ain't gotta blow a gasket, Harley. We get it from your pa'."

"I called him. He's not answering."

"Hardly ever," Holly said, pulling her curly black hair into a ponytail. "Just have to drive over yonder."

"Where?"

"Really, Harley? Cranston. Your mammaw's house. Right. Ms. Richards left him that nice-ass house, and you oughta see it now."

Harley was disappointed. She practically grew up in that house, and here was her screw-up of a father tarnishing good memories by taking the value of something wholesome and crapping on it.

"Okay, whatever," Harley said, refusing to allow such news to become her focal point. "I gotta go, but listen. I found your pa'."

Holly's expression dropped. "What?"

Harley explained everything that Freah relayed to her about their mother, Teddy Lee, and Randy Shivers. Harley then opened her photo gallery on her phone and showed Holly a picture of Randy's Facebook page.

"Call Mom. Make her ass tell you everything, hear?"

Holly nodded. "I will."

Harley hugged her. "I love you."

Holly's eyes watered. 'Love' was not a word that they commonly used in their family.

"I love you too."

Harley hurried out the door. The vast neighborhood of Cranston Brooke was all the way on the other side of town.

Holly grabbed her phone and pulled up Randy Shivers' Facebook page, and the first post was a photo of Randy and some man. The caption read, "Merle and me gone fishing."

Holly could see the resemblance, and it made her want to know more about Randy. Where was he now? Did he know about her? Does he have any more children? This has changed everything.

Chapter 25

Errol was seated in the back of the SUV beside Squirrel. Robin was driving as Freah and Billy wiped bullets clean of any possible prints before loading them into magazines—they were on their way to Cranston Brooke.

Squirrel lit a joint and the pungent smell of the cannabis quickly traveled throughout the vehicle.

Besides visiting Lee County for rival football games, Errol had never really ventured throughout the town before, but from what he could tell it appeared wholesome and old—a place that hadn't put forth much effort to advance beyond the post-war of World War II architecture.

"You gotta be a rotten turd to have your own daughter sleep with your enemy's son," Robin said.

Freah shook her head annoyingly. "Robin, shut the fuck up, will ya. That damn gal ain't done no such thang."

"It's like Merle said," Squirrel chimed, "Where's the point, right? Errol was not harmed. So if that was the case, what happened?"

"She got cold feet," Billy said.

"Or a warm heart," Squirrel countered.

Errol looked at his uncle.

"Love dictates eighty percent of the brain," Squirrel added, "Have ya' doing some of the stupidest shit in the world."

"Amen," Freah said, chuckling lightly. "And that gal love my baby. Saw it myself."

Errol smiled.

"So why run off the way she did?" Robin asked.

"Lotta times folks run because they don't have no one to run to," Squirrel answered. "*Thank* about the hot pot that gal was just thrown into, having to choose between her boyfriend and her pa'. Robin, you of all people should know how hard it is to choose cum over blood. When your folks came down on top of you for dating Billy, you nearly had a nervous breakdown."

"Nearly, my ass. She did have one," Billy said. "Especially once her pa' told her, 'If you taint my bloodline with the likes of a nigger, I'll hang ya' by ya' boots.'"

Errol looked surprised. He had no idea.

"And I made a choice, didn't I?" Robin expressed. "Lost everything for—"

"Love," Freah said, accepting the joint from Squirrel. "It's why we're all here. Me, Savannah, you. We had to make a choice, and when the time comes, so will Harley."

Errol was familiar with the basics of how his mother's parents disapproved of her being with his father, and he figured it was why his parents were so accepting of Harley—their love was interrupted, so they don't want to interrupt the fire of the probability that obviously exists between him and Harley.

"Love is war," Squirrel said.

Errol looked at him questionably.

"Only if it's abused," Freah said, exhaling.

Errol looked at her curiously.

"Even if it isn't, it's still a fight to stay in love," Billy pointed out.

Errol looked at him thoughtfully.

"But anythang worth fighting for has value," Robin offered.

Errol nodded. He didn't believe for one minute that Harley was playing a role for her father. She cared for him, and if Billy and Robin knew what all him and Harley have been through tonight, they wouldn't be so quick to judge her.

Errol couldn't explain the motive of why Harley decided to steal his truck or ignore his phone calls, but he trusted her—he had to, otherwise what they have is nothing.

And almost as if he thought her up, his phone rang. Looking at the screen, his heart stopped and he nearly dropped his phone in haste to press the 'SPEAKER' button.

"Baby," he said.

Squirrel cut his eyes to his nephew. Freah turned around in her seat. Robin looked in on him from the rearview mirror.

"Errol," Harley said, sobbing. "I'm sorry. Please don't hate me."

"Never. It's okay."

"I just wanna make it all right."

The tears in her voice crushed him, and he had to combat his own floodgate.

"How?" Errol asked her.

"I don't know. Talk some sense in 'em, tell 'em to stop all this mess," she sniffed. "Just . . . Just don't want to lose no one."

"I am your baby."

"Always."

"I'll fix this," she promised. "I love you."

"Harley, where are you?"

She hung up. He called her back—the line went straight to voicemail.

Freah sighed sadly. Whenever they thought that Teddy Lee had actually kidnapped Errol, her heart ached terribly, to the extent that she felt that she was going to die if anything bad had happened to him, and now here he was on a ride-along to a shitstorm. Merle and her have to do better by their children, because next time they may not be as fortunate as they were tonight.

To hell with the drug game. They have each other, and that's enough.

Chapter 26

The White family parked around the corner from the house in Cranston Brooke, and surveyed their surroundings before considering exiting their vehicles. This was ground zero—horrible lighting, cracked and uneven pavement, and homes that seemed to be losing their battle against time.

"There's a few choppers in the yard," Squirrel said, relaying what he saw when they drove past the house. "Blacked out windows. Ain't no floodlights or red L.E.D.s anywhere."

"I saw woods behind the house and some kinda shed," Billy said.

"Well, Dog Man said there's nine in the house, that's including him and Jaxon," Robin said. "Reckon it's gon' be a pretty even fight."

Squirrel grabbed a stick of dynamite from off his lap and looked at it, admiringly. "This here gon' change the count real quick."

"Better be careful with that shit, boy," Billy warned. "That could kill us all if ya don't know the fizzle on them fuses."

Squirrel shook his head. "The fizzle stick to poker, Billy, and let us real rustlers handle this, aight?"

Freah looked to her son. "So, you're stayin' out here with Rock-on, and if—"

Errol interrupted, his voice tinged with disappointment. "Yeah, I know, ma. Shoot 'em or call one of y'all." He shook his head. "I just don't know why I can't—"

"'Cause you ain't, and that's final."

Errol clamped his mouth shut.

They all got out the SUV, and Errol walked past Savannah to get into the car with Rock-on.

"How far is Merle out?" Lisette asked Freah.

"Not far."

Becka laid her M-16 against her shoulder, muttering, "Leave it to uncle Merle to be late to the cookout."

"Yeah," Squirrel agreed, putting a bullet in the head of his Desert Eagle. "Good thing it's my barbecue."

"What?" Freah gave him a confused look.

"We're goin'," was all Squirrel said, then he hopped in the driver's seat of the S.U.V.

Everyone exchanged looks like, 'What the fuck?' Then the engine roared to life. They couldn't let Squirrel run off half-cocked and botch the hit—or worse, get himself killed.

"Fuck," Freah muttered, her face twisted in irritation. "Let's go."

***

Jim Bob entered the living room from the restroom and reclaimed his seat on the sofa. Turbo passed him a loaded pipe of meth, and Jim Bob patted his pockets in search of his lighter.

"Teddy Lee came back in yet?" Jim Bob asked.

"Still out back. Chain-smoking like a condemned man," Nick answered.

"Reckon my daughter step out with a spook, I'd smoke a few packs too. Then go and kill 'em both," Ray shared.

Bruiser nodded. "Now that's poetic, son."

Starks took a gulp of his beer and so happened looked to the kitchen and saw Dog Man texting conspicuously on his phone. Starks nudged Turbo with his elbow to bring it to his attention.

***

Errol was sitting with his thoughts—staring blankly through the windshield. At the moment he didn't know what to say, what to feel, what to do.

"I'll be glad when this is all over with," Rock-on said.

Errol looked at his uncle. He loved Rock-on, always has; he was the fun one who knew how to get a party up and rolling, but this wasn't a party that he would willingly attend, so Rock-on's presence was not needed. He wasn't a killer, and that's who they were facing tonight—treacherous animals with long reach and merciless consistency for violent motives.

"Yeah," was all Errol said to Rock-on.

Errol looked back to the windshield just as his truck was turning onto the street. It sped past them.

"Harley," he said, hurrying to open his door.

"Errol, no," Rock-on said.

***

Squirrel was the first to enter the front yard of the house. Freah followed her brother-in-law, limping, gun ready to fire. The others trailed closely, watchfully, careful not to stumble over discarded tires, rusty lawn tools, and planks of weathered wood.

"Squirrel, no," Freah said tightly, stopping him from lighting the fuse of a stick of dynamite. "Put that shit away."

Squirrel sucked his teeth irritably but did as he was told. The two made their way toward the backyard.

Becka, Robin, Billy, and Lisette eased to the front door. The screen door was slightly ajar, and they all figured a hotdog to a doughnut that their rusty hinges were going to squeal like a wounded mammal.

"Shit," Becka murmured.

***

"Say boy, let me see that phone of yours," Turbo said to Dog Man as he and his boys approached the table.

Dog Man was hesitant. "What for?"

Bruiser smacked him.

"Hey!" Jaxon shouted, rising up from his chair.

Starks grabbed him by his throat and slammed his back against the wall.

Dog Man whipped his pistol out from underneath his shirt, and Jim Bob caught him by his wrist—Dog Man pulled the trigger and Ray yelped painfully.

***

Teddy Lee, with his foot propped up against the shed, lit a cigarette, then leaned his head back to view the universe. A plan that was expected to be as smooth as ice was becoming as choppy as the Tannenbaum Rapids in Appalachia, and it was pissing him off to the furthest extent of positivity, if that was ever a word.

Then a sound interrupted his thoughts, like the *crunch* of styrofoam—someone was walking alongside the house. Teddy Lee reached for his piece just when a gunshot rang from inside the house.

***

At the sound of the gunshot, Savannah swung the screen door wide and Billy kicked the door in. Becka and Lisette swept past Billy and entered the house with guns blazing.

***

Detecting the sound of violence inside the house, Freah and Squirrel exchanged a quick glance, then rushed around the side. As they veered into the opening of the backyard, they locked eyes with Teddy Lee, who immediately opened fire. Squirrel dropped to the ground from a headshot, and Freah staggered back while returning fire—missing Teddy Lee as he bolted toward the woods.

Then—

The back door came opened and Jim Bob and Ray scurried down the steps of the porch with the light of the living room cast upon them.

Freah shot Ray in his shoulder before Jim Bob turned his MAC-11 on her and laid heavy on the trigger. She dived to the side of the house.

***

Savannah and Becka helped Dog Man and Jaxon up to their feet—they were both wounded, shot in the lower region of their bodies—so was Robin.

Turbo, Nick, Bruiser, and Starks were all dead. The walls were riddled with bullet holes and the cherry of a cigarette was licking at the hem of a curtain.

"Billy, get them to the car," Lisette said while taking a quick observation of the wound in Jaxon's thigh. "Keep pressure on it, hear?" she instructed her son.

Then Lisette, Savannah, and Becka all ran for the back door, where they saw Freah down on her knees firing into the woods.

"Is that Squirrel?" Savannah asked as Freah fired her last bullet.

"He's dead," Freah said, pain laced in her tone.

"What!" Becka, Savannah, and Lisette all exclaimed simultaneously. "No!"

Freah inserted another magazine. "Let's get them motherfuckers."

The White girls dashed across the yard.

***

Harley leapt out the cab of the truck with a firm grip on the rifle. Gunshots were erupting at the rear of the house, but movement in her peripheral vision snagged her attention. She swung the rifle to her left—inches from squeezing the trigger.

"Harley, don't shoot!"

Harley's heart stuttered. It was Errol. Dropping the rifle, she leapt into his arms and yelped, "Baby."

"It's on fire," came a voice. "Hurry."

Errol and Harley both looked toward the front door of the house and saw people exiting hastily—obviously fleeing from something or someone.

"Ah, Billy, you gonna push me down, dammit," said a voice that Errol recognized as Robin.

"It's my family," Errol told Harley. "Come on."

They ran to the aid of the wounded just when the house exploded in a rush of fire and debris. Errol dived to take Harley to the ground as Dog Man, Jaxon, and Billy all sailed overhead in a frisbee-like manner. Robin, completely engulfed in flames, escaped to the yard with her arms flailing wildly about, screaming—inhaling flames that were singeing her lungs.

The caked-up chemicals that were on the walls from cooking meth were ignited by the fire.

***

Savannah entered the woods behind Becka and Lisette, but quickly lost sight of them in the gloom. Gaping over her shoulder, she saw Freah hobbling as fast as she could to catch up to them.

A shot cracked in the woods, but before she could look in the direction in which it came, the house went up like a match tip.

Froooomm!

***

Errol helped Harley up from the ground, speaking over the slight *"Diiiiinng"* in his ears.

"Baby, you alright?" he asked.

Harley looked down at herself. "Yeah. Yeah, I thank so," she answered, her tone distant like a person who was trying to figure something out.

They looked to the inferno as a series of painful wails rushed toward them—someone was trampling throughout the yard while on fire.

"Oh my God," Harley said, covering her mouth with her hand.

Errol quickly removed his coat and Harley followed suit; while running to smother the flames of the burning victim, multiple gunshots rang out. Harley looked toward the woods, which was a dense area of the property that she knew like the back of her hand, but so did her father.

Errol tossed his coat over the head of the victim and Harley used hers to tackle the person to the ground, but at that exact moment, the person went completely still.

"No, no, no, no, no, no, no," Errol continuously said as they feverishly worked to smother the fire. "No!"

The person was seared beyond recognition. Smoke drifted from the body and the smell was unbearable.

"Robin," Billy said, collapsing to his knees near her body. "Baby?" he cried. "Baby?"

"I'm sorry," Harley said before turning to run away.

"Harley!" Errol called after her.

She knelt to grab hold of the rifle, then bolted to the woods—she didn't have the slightest idea what she was doing, but she just knew that she had to do something.

"Harley!" called Errol.

She kept running.

***

Freah entered the woods with precaution. A gunshot rang and she flinched—swinging her gun left. The darkness was working against her, on top of her injuries at that, so her odds were in the shitter. She moved deeper into the woods, dragging her foot. Then she paused. Someone was running; the patter of shoes grew louder and louder. Freah aimed here, aimed there, then a heavy hand grabbed hold of her shoulder.

***

Ray saw a dark figure running in his direction and swiftly slipped behind a tree.

"One Mississippi. Two Mississippi," he quietly counted. "Three."

Then he sprang out on his possible pursuer, taking them by surprise. Just as their features passed through a stream of moonlight, Ray saw that it was a woman and not an Infidel—a free kill.

Ray swatted her gun from her hand, grabbed her by her throat, and forced her backward until she slammed into a tree.

"Stupid bitch," he said through clenched teeth, then headbutted her—again and again, breaking her nose before. . .

"Night, night," came a voice.

Ray had enough time to cut his eyes to his left before Savannah blew his brains out of his head. Becka fell on her knees, gasping for air as blood poured from her nostrils.

"You okay?" Savannah asked her.

Gunshots. One, two, three!

Savannah looked over her shoulder just as Jim Bob fell to his death, and standing there, shaking like a leaf on a tree, was Rock-on.

“Baby?” Savannah said, uncertain if her eyes were deceiving her or not.

“He was . . . He was—he was gonna shoot you,” Rock-on stammered, staring down at Jim Bob’s body blankly. “I couldn’t let ’em, let ’em do . . .” his words trailed off.

Savannah carefully relieved her husband of the gun. “You did right, baby. It’s okay,” she said, hugging him to ease his nerves.

“I heard all that shooting.”

“Uh-huh,” she said, caressing the back of his head.

“Then,” he swallowed, “The—the house blew up, and I—and I just, just . . .”

“Right, I know, sweety,” she said, then pulled back to look into his eyes. “Thank you.” Then she kissed him.

Lisette appeared—breathless but well intact. “Ya'll got ’em,” she said before averting her attention to Becka and asking, “Who did it?”

Becka nodded to Ray’s body and Lisette kicked him in his face—dead or not, don’t no one fuck with her children.

***

After helping Dog Man, Billy, and Jaxon into his truck, Errol peeled off towards the woods, spewing chunks of earth from the rear tires. Sirens were singing in the distance, but Errol wasn’t leaving without the others. Speeding alongside the fire, he looked over at Dog Man who was suffering from intense pain.

“Hold in there, hear?” Errol said. “We’re getting the hell outta here.”

Spotting a wide enough opening for the width of his truck, Errol cut the wheel to the right and bumbled over some uneven terrain that only got rougher as they entered the woods.

Coming to a halt, Errol grabbed the 9mm that his mother gave him and said, "Y'all hang tight." Then he hopped out of the truck.

"I'm coming with you," said Billy.

***

Teddy Lee whirled Freah around by her shoulder and smacked the dog shit out of her. Blood flew from her lip and she fell against a tree—losing hold of her gun. Dazed, she struggled to maintain her balance.

"Gout-mouth bitch," Teddy Lee said, punching her in her jaw, dropping her to her knees—a dislocation that caused that side of her face to sag and swell almost immediately. "I don't lose, nigger."

Drawing his pistol from the waistline of his jeans, he aimed it dead center.

"No!" someone shouted, tackling Teddy Lee from behind.

Harley rolled away from her father and recovered her rifle. Teddy Lee reached for his gun, but Harley fired a round into the ground near his hand and he pulled back cautiously—a shot that caught the attention of everyone in the woods.

"Pa', enough," Harley said. "This shit has gone too far."

Showing his teeth like the wolf he is, Teddy Lee said, "Bitch, you got some fucking nerve showing up here after the shit you did."

Harley's eyes watered. It hurt to hear him talk to her in that manner. "Stop, please."

He shouted, "A nigger?" His tone burned with emotion. "You're just like your no-good ass mother." He looked at Freah. "Worthless as this black monkey."

"Stop," Harley cried.

"I'll stop when your nigger-loving ass is—"

Harley cut him off. "I do love him. And nothing you do will change that. You—"

Teddy Lee grabbed his gun.

"Pa', stop!" she warned him, but it fell upon deaf ears.

He swung the gun to shoot Freah just when Errol and Billy appeared from out of nowhere—sliding to a halt from running, Errol hollered, "Noooo!"

Teddy Lee quickly redirected his aim. Errol threw his arms up to shield his face. Freah dove for her gun. Billy grabbed Errol by the collar of his shirt, yanking him out of the line of fire. But before Teddy Lee could pull the trigger, a shot rang out, and a slug hit Teddy Lee square in the chest—right in the heart.

Errol, Freah, and Billy all turned to look at Harley, who was still holding the rifle at chin level—wisps of smoke curling from the chamber and barrel.

Becka, Rock-on, Savannah, and Lisette emerged from the darkness, and Errol had to quickly stop them from raising their guns toward Harley.

"She's with us," he quickly said.

The wail of sirens snapped Harley out of her trance. Lowering the rifle, but eyes still set on her father's body, she said, "We gotta go. I know the backwoods leads to the highway."

Fade To Black . . .

Chapter 27

14 Months Later

It's been over a year since everything kicked off, and all of the survivors have changed in one way or another. At some point in their lives, a drug dealer finds themselves slung between a rock and a hard place—at a point of no return. If they don't fight back, they could lose their lives, either to violence or a trumped-up federal case—a sentence that starts with a letter, not a number: LIFE. Normally, the low point of making fast money is destructive, but some make it out victorious, like the White family did, though at a tremendous cost. The death of Squirrel and Robin. The paralysis of Davie. The raw exposure of murder and its lasting impact on the mind. Trying to find peace becomes an ongoing mental battle because the blood they've spilled can never be washed away—it haunts them. So, the showdown wasn't the White family's final face-off. Every day, they have to look themselves in the mirror and face the real opposition—their past.

At this moment, the doors of their lives open wide for all to enter, for all to witness the outcome of the Whites, as the enchanting song "Love" by Trin-I-Tee 5:7 plays softly in the background of these current events.

Merle & Freah

Merle and Freah posed for a selfie with the breathtaking features of Niagara Falls in the background. In the company of their two youngest children, whom they were homeschooling, Freah and Merle were living life on the road—belting country songs while traveling their great nation in their shiny black $350,000 RV.

Norton was no longer home for Freah and Merle, and the life they had led was far behind them. If there was one thing Teddy Lee had taught them, it was that love will always prevail in the end. It has to—if not, it'll all be for nothing.

Merle catered to her inner needs.

Freah fed his insatiable sexual appetite.

Merle triggered her playful, creative side.

Freah ignited his zestful quality.

They completed each other.

Love isn't about turning an entire 360, because a 360 only forms a circle, where two people would simply end up where they started. True love is a 180, which forms the letter "C," standing for change, companionship, compatibility, commitment, communication, comfort, confirmation—but more importantly, completeness. There is no greater achievement than having access to the whole shebang, for love is greater than money or God, because without it, one could not value either wholeheartedly.

Davie

Davie's wife, Katherine, pushed him through Union Park in downtown Norton. The day was perfect—82 degrees with a light breeze that traveled down from the mountains.

It had been over a year since Davie was paralyzed from the waist down, and since then, he had gained over 130 pounds. The once overly buff brawler was now only a shadow of his former self. Did it hurt him to lose his ability to walk? Absolutely. But only for the three-month period that followed. The word of God spoke to him personally, uplifting and cleansing his soul to the point where he could say, "A devil may have taken my legs, but my God gave me my wings." Davie had surrendered his life to Christ and met an incredible woman in Bible study who had completely fulfilled his heart.

Merle, along with the newly appointed Sheriff Maddy Smith, tampered with the evidence to ensure that Davie walked free from the murder charges. God is good all the time, and Davie has learned to let Jesus take the wheel. The results have brought him peace, joy, and purpose.

Katherine and Davie stopped at a bench so she could take a load off. They talked while watching a frisbee football game. The simple life. He loved it.

Rock-on & Savannah

Tiny Men was a 30,000 sq. ft. hoorah of total masculinity. Wrestling, boxing, karate, fitness training, simulated shooting programs, auto mechanic courses, sex education, and much more. Rock-on's business offered boys from ages 15-21 the lessons of a father they were most likely growing up without.

With the help of his business partner, Savannah, Tiny Men was structured to mold adolescent boys into not only physically strong men but also mentally solid enough to become breadwinners—teaching them social etiquette, ethical practices, financial management, and more.

Rock-on and Savannah were standing ringside, watching a sparring match. They employed over sixty people who carried out various tasks and taught their professional skills to the boys, making Tiny Men a place full of grunts, pants, yelps, the tap-tap-tap of punching bags, and weights falling to the floor, just to name a few. The second floor, however, was mostly classrooms and Savannah and Rock-on's office.

Savannah looked away from the bout and at Rock-on. She was finally happy. She and Rock-on had not only renewed their wedding vows in Honolulu, Hawaii, but these days, they were inseparable. The fear of losing her that night in those woods had opened his eyes to how important she was to him. Now, he was all hers—no more flings or long-term affairs.

Rock-on looked at her.

"I love you," she said.

"I love you more."

She laughed. "Impossible."

Rock-on took her hand. "Nothing's impossible."

They walked across the floor toward the door. That night in the woods had made Rock-on more appreciative of his beautiful wife—and had also made him a man.

When the law came knocking for answers about Jessica Laney and the accident at the Gladdison Motel involving Savannah's Toyota Camry, she told them, "My husband and me got into a big ol' fight that night, and I went to her trailer to stay the night, 'cause her and me were good friends like that, ya' know? But I needed some things from the house, like my work uniform, so Jessica took my car and never came back."

So far, so good.

Dog Man & Lisette

Lisette was sitting at a table in the visiting room of Keen Mountain Prison, awaiting to see her husband. On the table were several food items that Lisette had purchased from the vending machines.

She eyed a couple standing against a backdrop of a yellow brick road, taking a photograph. She and Dog Man had taken many photos together in the six months since his incarceration. The conflict between them, the Infidels, and Dougherty had drawn the attention of law enforcement from far and wide. As soon as word got out that Dog Man was alive, he was immediately arrested for the murder of Gene Dougherty and implicated as an accessory to the Lee County killings that Squirrel supposedly orchestrated after his daring jailbreak. However, after a thorough search of Teddy Lee's house, once Dog Man had submitted his innocence, the sledgehammer was recovered from inside the hallway closet, with traces of Gene's dried blood where the handle met the steel. The handle was also covered in Teddy Lee's fingerprints.

Dog Man and Merle had just installed the camera inside his truck that morning, which was a last-minute idea of Merle's that ended up saving Dog Man's life. However, he couldn't beat the charge of faking his own death and was sentenced to the maximum penalty of 42 months.

"I escaped," Dog Man told the detectives in the interrogation room. "But I came back, because, ya know, I just couldn't leave Gene like that. But when I made it back up the mountain, he was dead. And that's when I did it. Figured if Teddy Lee thought I was dead, he wouldn't come looking for me."

Merle had Billy call the Norton Sheriff's Department to report Robin missing. He was told that she had to be missing for 24 hours or more before a report could be filed.

"Well, by God, I ain't stupid, lady. I know that. Why the Sam hell you think I waited to call you?" Billy told the desk sergeant.

Merle knew it would take days, maybe even longer, to successfully identify Robin's remains. By Billy reporting her missing well before her discovery, it would exclude his possible involvement in the Lee County killings.

Dog Man walked through the door, and Lisette smiled. He was her king, and she couldn't wait for this to be over so they could move on with their lives.

She stood up from her chair and planted a deep kiss on his lips. He palmed her ass cheeks.

"Break it up," a C.O. ordered.

Lisette and Dog Man shot the officer an annoyed look before sitting back down.

Lisette began opening Dog Man's food and making a plate as she caught him up on what was going on with their kids and their newly opened gas station, *Dog House*.

She fed him a hot wing, then took it upon herself to lick the buffalo sauce off of his lips.

The couple ate, laughed, and enjoyed each other's company. Real love is patient, and in situations like theirs, that patience is tested. In that very visiting room, many women would fail by giving into another man behind their mate's back. But Lisette was not a weak, sexually driven skank—she was married and committed to much more than just a night in the sack. W.I.F.E. (Willingly In Forever Ever).

Errol & Harley

"I'm here, baby, I'm here," Errol said, holding onto Harley's hand.

"Oh, goddamn. Shit, shit, shit," Harley continuously muttered, perspiring and breathing heavily.

"Push for me, Harley," Dr. Simmons instructed, spotting the fetus's head.

A diamond wedding ring glimmered on Harley's finger, and on her forearm, in bold red letters, was *'White Girl'*.

Harley's life with Errol was grand. His parents had given them their ranch as a wedding present, and they'd configured the place to their liking. However, there had been dark moments, where the images of her father and that night in the woods haunted her. But over time, she was getting better. She was finally grasping the fact that he was not her father at all. No real man could ever muster the audacity to turn his back on his child, let alone kill his own creation over something as trivial as dating someone outside of his race. Only ignorance judges what it doesn't know.

"It's a boy!" Simmons said.

Harley cracked a small grin and said weakly, "A White boy."

Standing outside the delivery room with her grandmother was Holly. She lived in Norton now with her father's family, who had immediately accepted her after she gathered the courage to contact them. The problem was, her father and his wife were missing, but Holly was determined to find out where he was. There was someone in Norton who knew something about his whereabouts.

She finally had a family who loved and accepted her for who she was—Black—and that meant everything to her.

Becka

Becka was house-sitting for Errol and Harley. Suffering from the munchies and craving some lemon sugar cookies, Becka hopped up onto the counter to flip through the pages of a cookbook she found inside a box in the pantry.

Becka was a wholesome country gal who preferred home-cooked meals over pizza or fast food. Plus, the fridge and the cupboards were stocked to the gills, so it was nonsense to waste her money.

Her phone rang. Looking over at the screen, she saw that it was her brother, Jaxon, calling. She ignored the call. He most likely either wanted to borrow some money or bother her about hooking him up with her friend Amber. Becka went back to her search for the ingredients for the sugar cookies—hopefully, the book had it in the baking section.

Jaxon called again, and she waved it off. He was a pain in the ass these days. Ever since that night he was shot, he'd adopted this tough-guy act that was starting to get on her nerves. Jaxon and their father were both fortunate to receive non-life-threatening injuries that didn't require hospitalization—through-and-through shots that Jaxon was amplifying as fatal wounds.

"Please. I've damaged more on a skateboard," Becka told Jaxon just yesterday.

A folded sheet of loose-leaf paper fell out of the cookbook and onto the floor. Becka leapt to her feet to retrieve it, and for no particular reason at all, she decided to read it.

Her eyes stretched wide. "Well, hell fire," she murmured.

It was Merle's recipe.

Chapter 28

Trinidad . . . 2 Months Later

The carnival was pulsating with life, and Freah and Merle danced in the street to a calypso band with the native folks. The true nature of the locals as they paraded in traditional costumes was exhilarating—the most astounding street party ever!

While bypassing decayed gingerbread-style villas, wooden huts, and rusty fences, Freah was twerking with the best of them. To visit Trinidad was her idea. Since she was a young girl, she has always wanted to visit the Caribbean, and now she was here with the love of her life and no children to monitor—a Baecation!

Merle took a gulp of rum from a large brown oval-shaped bottle, then looked up to the crisp blue sky and released an energetic *"Hoorah"* to emphasize the intense burning sensation of the liquor.

Life was grand—no worries. But there were times that he wished that Squirrel was still alive. He missed that crazy sonofabitch.

Merle looked past a neo-gothic Cathedral, and just beyond some old trees at the water—Squirrel would have surely been occupied with one of them jet skis right now, racing about like a madman. The thought of Squirrel running people over made Merle chuckle.

Coconut palms waved gently in the breeze, and the delicious aroma of callaloo soup and crab boasted broadly as the party progressed toward where the forest met the sea.

Freah and Merle danced provocatively down a beaten path of packed clay and rocks, shards of pottery, and high stands of bamboo. They felt as though they were on their honeymoon. A colorful sisseroy parrot landed on Merle's shoulder, and he nearly leapt out of his skin. Freah laughed at her husband's initial state of fear—Merle yelped and swatted his hand wildly at the sizable bird.

Merle smiled and said to her, "Ha ha. Real funny."

"And it was. Thank you very much," she replied.

They kissed.

Kissed some more.

It was like they were teenagers again. The fire was burning hot and they wanted to rip each other's clothes off.

"How 'bout we cut this short and head back to the room?" Freah said, pussy throbbing.

"Now that's the best idea you've had all . . ."

Merle's phone rang. Reaching inside his back pocket for his device, he gave Freah a look that said, *Hold that thought.* Merle saw that it was his cousin, Cassandra, calling from Atlanta. He hadn't seen or spoken to her since Squirrel and Robin's funeral.

"It's Cassy," he told Freah.

Freah smiled. Cassandra was one of her favorite in-laws. Before Cassandra decided to up and leave Norton for the big city, her and Freah were inseparable. But that was long ago.

Merle answered the call. "Cassy, hey. What's—"

"Merle, they killed my babies!" Cassandra shrieked. Her teary voice was saturated in pain.

"Oh lord, why? Why, why, why?"

"These mothafuckas," she shouted, then her tone dropped a few decibels. "Killed my babies, Merle. I need you here, now." She broke down, screaming curses to God. "You mothafucka!"

Freah saw the immediate change in her husband. Something was wrong.

"Merle?" Freah asked. "Baby, what's—"

"I'm on my way," Merle said into the phone. "I'm not in the country right now, Cassy, but I'm-ma book a—"

"Merle, I want this city burnt to the fucking ground."

Merle's nostrils flared and his heart drummed against his ribcage as a spike of anxiety heightened his breathing.

Freah took hold of his hand. Concern was etched deeply in her features, and as she continued to listen to the one-sided exchange between Merle and Cassandra, she began to feel the urge of murder arising in the center of her chest.

Merle ended the call. "We're leaving," he said tightly. "Get us a flight, now." By her hand, he led Freah back to the street.

Freah quickly retrieved her phone from her back pocket, asking, "What happened?"

"Some sidewinding sumbitches killed Cassy's children."

Pulling her hand free of his hold, Freah said with an incredulous expression, "What? No."

Merle looked over his shoulder at her. "We're going to Atlanta," he said.

Freah's expression tightened and she hurried past him, saying, "You damn right we are." She dialed the number of the airport.

Merle trailed behind his wife, who was rudely shoving people aside as she spoke on the phone. He was deeply saddened by this. His cousin was too hysterical to explain the exact details of the incident to him, but the pain in her voice told him everything that he needed to know. It told him that someone has to die.

Chapter 29

Atlanta, Georgia…

Sycamore Baptist was a red-roofed church with a number of magnificent qualities. The stone structure was nested amongst the most luxurious homes on West Paces Ferry Rd. in Buckhead. Eye-snagging pottery and a statuary courtyard of known biblical figures who overlooked a holy fountain of faith. Artsy stainless glass windows that revealed the story of Jesus and his disciples. Exquisite.

The afternoon was bleak – a deep gray sky with a nasty storm brewing on the horizon, so the air smelled of the rain that was scheduled to arrive shortly.

Merle was hanging in the rear of the parking lot – leaning against the driver side door of his rental car smoking a cigarette. The funeral was letting out. Merle watched as people hugged one another and formed circles for last minute discussions before departing to their respected vehicles. The White family had really taken a hit this time – with the tragic loss of Squirrel and Robin, and now this – seven family members . . . gone . . . forever.

Merle saw his cousin Cassy exit the church with Freah. Cassy was a bluster of tears and Freah had to hold her firmly by her arm to keep her from falling to her knees.

Growing up Merle and Cassy were very close, and he remember the day when she visited the farm with the news of her moving to Atlanta. She was so exited, but Merle wasn't one bit pleased with her decision to abandon Norton and the family. Country folks weren't built for city life – it normally swallowed them whole then spit them out onto a curb of woes and regrets, and that's exactly what happened – a devastating blow that Cassy will never recover from. Two of her adult children, along with her six grandchildren were lying inside of coffins – a closed casket affair with very little clarity as to why this happened.

Cassy's eldest daughter, Eboni, was currently in ICU at Grady Hospital fighting to resurface from a bullet-induced coma. Eboni was the only person who could've possibly shined a hint of light about that fatal night at her backyard barbecue. A festive gathering to welcome her sister Tink home from a long tour of running from her past.

Merle keyed in on Errol and Harley. They had a son now and were forming a family of their own. The deadly incident against Teddy Lee and his gang was still fresh, and by no means did they deserve another chaotic scenario such as this one to come. But Merle on the other hand – as much as he wanted peace, has to see this through – someone has to answer for this shit.

Savannah, Rock-on, and Davie were all talking to Rick, who was a relative from Washington DC. Rick was the leader of the notorious *Bumpy Knuckle Cartel*, and they were known for raising Cain all up through the eastern seaboard. Their brand of crazy will surely come in handy – Atlanta was about to burn from vengeance.

The last time that the White family came together like this was at Squirrel's and Robin's funeral, which was truly sad, but also a stern reminder that death was upon them quite frequently. Something has to change.

Merle noticed that Tink didn't exit the church with all of the others. He flicked his cigarette into the grass, then walked to the doors of Sycamore Baptist. He had never been much of a suit type of guy – a pair of worn Levi's and a clean white t-shirt suited him just fine in life, so the black suit that he was currently wearing was choking him in a sense, he felt awkward, like a walking billboard for an insurance firm or oil gig.

Merle was a simple man with the most difficult life. Leadership required courage, brains, and a heap full of sacrifice, and he had given his all to his family and not an ounce to himself. Some men would say that he was crazy, and in return he would most likely agree. "Crazy enough to cut your goddamn throat, you sumbitch. Now cross one of mines and see, would ya'," is how he would've put it.

Entering the church, Merle saw Tink sitting in a front pew. Her head was hung low in the manner of a person who was enduring great sorrow. Tink had always been Merle's favorite. Which was his little secret, because he certainly loved all of Cassy's children, but Tink was just a tad bit more adorable and humorous as a child than any of the others were. So, her grief weighed heavy upon his heart.

He made his way down the aisle. The caskets were perfectly aligned with large photographs of the deceased that were position on easels with bouquets of white roses at the foot of the wooden posts. Tink's only child was amongst the others, and Merle imagined that it was hard for her to leave him to the care of God. It'll been hard for anyone really, so he took slow strides, hating to oppose on the moment.

Tink was present at the night of shooting. Her and her son Marquise had just arrived in Atlanta hours before the incident from New York, but neither of the two never imagined that it would be their last time ever seeing one another.

Merle took a seat alongside of Tink and placed his arm across her shoulders to pulled her close to him. Her body shuddered in his grasp.

"I can't take it," she cried. "I can't—I can—I'm not gonna be okay," she stammered, then paused as if in search of the right words. "I want my baby back." Her agony heightened.

Merle didn't say a word. It wasn't that he didn't want to console her, but more so that he didn't know what to say.

How does one tell someone who just lost their child to a bullet that it's going to be okay? That life goes on? That the pain will eventually settle?

A long minute pasted.

Then Tink stood up from the pew to pace the floor. She was a jittery mess. "I want em' to pay, Merle." She looked into his eyes. "All of them."

They had very little to go on about the shooting. Outside of the actual footage that revealed four masked gunmen and the name who Seneca whispered into Tink's ear before taking his last breath, the trail went cold.

Seneca was Cassy's only son and youngest of her bunch. He was a rough neck with ties to some pretty bad people, and before his eyes went cloudy and his soul escaped to the atmosphere, he said these words. "Amir did this."

Amir.

Four gunmen.

One dark night.

"We'll get em' Tink," Merle said reassuringly." As sure as shit stank, we'll have 'em by their ankles. Rick has—"

She cut him off. "No. No, not Rick. Too messy, too loud. Momma said you'll know how to finesse this."

Merle furrowed a brow. "Say what you mean, Tink."

Killing these fuckers isn't enough, Merle. That does nothing for me. I want them to suffer. Suffer just as much as I am, right now, dammit. I wanna put em' in a cage like the fucking animals they are," her tone sizzled with anger and pain, "and watch them die slowly. But I need your help to do it. No *wild wild west* shit like Rick be on, 'cause that's what they'll expect."

"Well, what do you have in mind?" he asked carefully.

Tink shrugged. "I don't know, I mean, I do, but . . . I guess we find out who all was involved and why, then pin their asses to the cross." She looked down at her hands and it put Merle in the mind of when she was a girl and was getting bullied by a girl named, Roxanne – Tink was broken.

"Momma said that you are the brains of our family and that you'll know exactly how to find these bastards and corner them into a hole."

With a sigh, Merle said. "So, you wanna put them in the can?"

"No. I wanna put them under it. I want them to watch everything and everyone that they love wither a fucking away."

Tink was a cop – the one person in their family who had always flown straight, so her request didn't surprise Merle one bit; he actually expected it. It made him think about Sheriff Dougherty and how he locked that sonofabitch away alongside of his family. He understood such grounds of revenge, quite well.

"You don't have much faith in your people?" he asked her, referring to the police department, because although Tink was not enrolled on the Atlanta Police Force, Merle knew that they were still treating her as if she was one of their own. A cop thing.

Tink scoffed. "Please. These cops down here got their heads up their asses. We have to do this ourselves, Merle."

Merle nodded. "Then let's get to work."

They heard the doors of the church open. Merle looked over his shoulder and saw, Cassy, Freah, Rick, Rock-on, Savannah, Errol, Harley, and Davie all entering in a single file line – wet from the sudden downpour that washed upon the roof with a peaceful roar.

Tink looked to her mother whose mascara was running down her pretty face. "We're gonna get em', momma," she told her. "And we're gonna get 'em good."

Cassy nodded approvingly, then looked to Merle for confirmation. "Cousin?"

Merle nodded. "Reckon we'll hit the trail of a snake in search of its nest."

Davie disapproved. The new found Christian inside of him would not allow him to participate in such behavior as of murder. "Now y'all hold on, a'ight. There's no sense in getting ourselves in no cock fight. It's not the way of the good book, Merle."

"Like hell it ain't. An eye for an eye is God's words, isn't it?" Rick chimed.

"That's the Old Test—"

Freah cut Davie off. "No time for a conscious, Davie. So I reckon it's best you just go home."

Davie looked to everyone, and he saw that they all agreed with Freah. "Don't do this. This can only worsen things y'all," he urged.

"It can't get no worse than it already is, Davie," Tink said. "We're going forward with this. Sorry."

"Then God bless Atlanta." Davie said sadly.

Then this happened . . .

Chapter 30

Months After The Funeral…

Amir awoke with a start. Someone was knocking at the front door like a fucking madman. Amir's vision was frizzy, fuzzy, like a television with horrible reception. As he blinked the cobwebs aside, his brain slowly processed his surroundings. He was in his bedroom, but he didn't recall the moment of ever lying down—or doing anything else, for that matter.

Natural light poured through the windows. Amir questioned the whereabouts of the curtains, as well as the hour of the day. The bedroom was warm and stuffy. Was the thermostat on the brink again? And what the hell was that sound . . . a lawn mower? Motorcycle? Power generator?

"Police. Open up!" came a voice.

Amir's eyes shot to the bedroom door. The first thought that came to his mind was, *Someone set me up.*

He quickly sat up in bed but was overtaken by nausea and extreme dizziness. Had he come down with the flu? Covid-19? In his 28 years of living, Amir had rarely ever gotten sick, so this current state of discomfort was questionable—just like the taste of stale liquor. He didn't drink. Then there was that smell, a coppery, almost metallic odor that literally seemed to come from nowhere. Amir was a certified gangster. The blood of his opps had dripped from his hands and smelled very similar to what he was sensing right now. Was he wounded? Why was there no indication of pain?

Closing his eyes, he fought to gather his bearings. Where was Alexandria? And why was the law at their door?

Amir wiped his eyes. Looking to the other side of the bed, his heart leapt into his throat.

"No!" his thoughts screamed, a rush of panic surging through him.

His long-time girlfriend was seated against the headboard with a butcher knife jammed into the side of her neck. *Dead.*

"Atlanta Police Department!" Amir heard, then the front door of the house crashed open. The splintery crack of the wood caused Amir to flinch.

Gaping down at himself—naked and covered in blood—Amir's chest tightened. What happened here? He would've never harmed a hair on Alexandria's head. Why couldn't he remember anything?

Amir looked at the wall. Scrawled above the headboard in blood were the words: *Better off dead.*

Amir shook his head—he wasn't about to go out like this. Turning on the balls of his feet to retrieve his pistol from his bedside drawer, he nudged a black duffel bag with his foot. Staring down at the bag strangely, Amir wondered if he and Alexandria had gotten into a fight. Did she pack the bag to leave?

Thunderous footsteps treaded up the stairs—they were coming for him. Amir reached for the handle of the drawer, but then he paused hesitantly. *Don't do it!* screamed the voice in his head.

Amir looked at Alexandria. A tear fell from the corner of his eye and rolled down the cheek of his face—amongst his beard. Lost, as he was.

The bedroom door flung open, and one cop said dramatically, "Jesus Christ."

Amir raised his hands above his head. "I didn't do this," he said, lowering himself to his knees. "I want my lawyer."

An officer cuffed Amir. A second cop knelt to inspect the contents of the duffel bag.

"Oh my God," said the second cop, combating the urge to vomit.

Amir looked over his shoulder to view the contents as well. The sight of the bloody fetus sickened him.

"Get this animal out of my sight," ordered a third officer. "Now!"

"I wouldn't do no shit like this."

"Tell it to the judge, asshole."

"Get them paramedics in here."

Chapter 31

The hotel suite was comfortably cool and scented by cinnamon potpourri. It was a quarter past three, 4th of July, and the orgy was well underway.

Petra McCawley, a prestigious judge in the Atlanta judicial system, was riding a big black juicy dick while deep-throating seven inches of girth. Her milky white cheeks clapped loudly against the escort's thighs—his 12" dick touching the bottom of her soul—it hurt so good. Drool was hanging from her chin as the white man fucked her face and pulled on her hair, slutting her out as she requested.

"Eat all of that dick, you filthy whore," he said.

Regina Bourke, of Wilmer, Doyen & Bourke law firm, was positioned on all fours on top of the coffee table, shouting, "Harder! Harder! Like that, yes, yes!" as a massive white cock slammed in and out of her moist asshole. Her voluptuous chocolate-colored breasts swung to and fro, long nipples grazing against the marble table—teasing her. Raising a hand while still perfectly balanced on the other, Regina reached past her navel to finger-fuck her pink wet pussy.

"Shit," she moaned pleasurably. "Mama like," her eyes rolled into the back of her head. "Fuck that ass right," she huffed. "You fucker."

Numa Espey, who was the gracious host of the gathering, walked the floor of the suite in a white Dior Haute satin gown that hugged her wide hips provocatively. Her petite, pedicured feet were strapped in a glittery pair of Louis

Vuitton stiletto heels—she had come a long way from wearing Nike Dunks and hair bonnets.

Raising her wine flute to her lips, Numa took a sip of Cabernet Sauvignon and savored the richness of black grapes.

Mayor Robinson, who was standing near the mini-bar, pulled his dick free of a whore's mouth and jizzed all over her face.

"Ugh, shit, fuck yeah," he grunted while stroking his long black rod.

Numa snapped her fingers and called the name of one of her girls. A half-naked Asian goddess hurried across the floor.

"Yes, madame?" said the woman.

Numa pointed down to the whore who was receiving the massive facial and said, "Heighten that demonstration, bitch."

The Asian beauty nodded, then knelt and proceeded to lick all over the ho's face before tongue-kissing the bitch with a mouthful of nut—driving the mayor crazy!

"I'll see your ten thousand," Dr. Crawford said at the poker table, "and raise you fifteen."

Perkins, a local politician and entrepreneur, stared across the table at Crawford—questioning a bluff. "Call," Perkins finally said.

Numa continued across the room, stepping over or around discarded clothing, or briefly overlooking a sexually perversed act that made her pussy twitch—that freaky shit turned her on. But there was only one man who could match her sexual energy. Amir.

"It's too big, I can't take it, take it out!" came a feminine voice from the central staircase. "No, put it back, put it back, but slow. Ah, fuck."

Pleasurable moans swelled as motorized sex toys hummed and buzzed. Percocets, Xanax bars, Molly, and booze were being fed to the guests moderately as recreational enhancements—on the house.

The floor-to-ceiling glass met a dropped column of gypsum wallboard. The Westin Peachtree Plaza Hotel was a five-star hospice that housed top-dollar customers such as celebrities, oil tycoons, top political figures, speakers of deliberative assemblies, and more. A place where Numa's brand of clientele aren't looked at twice or suspected of any shenanigans.

Standing at the glass, Numa stared at the urban sprawl of downtown Atlanta. She loved her city—a true Rican Mama from the east side.

Numa has had a hard life. Her father and mother had high hopes of abandoning a poverty-stricken existence in Puerto Rico in exchange for the American dream, but only experienced a Federal nightmare in the end.

Numa's father, Roberto, had landed a maintenance job at Knights Inn motel on Bouldercrest Road. After several months of proving that he was not only a hard worker, but also trustworthy and dependable, Mr. Caldwell, the owner and a fairly decent man—from what Numa could remember of him—promoted Roberto to night manager. Upon happily accepting the glorious position, Roberto immediately hired his wife as a maid. The money wasn't all too great, but they managed financially in subsidized housing and public transit. Once Numa was born, her mother, Calisa, was eligible for welfare, but Roberto was a proud man with old-fashioned beliefs—he would hear nothing of it. So with a third mouth to feed, the struggle became a vice that was latched onto their throats—a dire situation in which Numa's parents knew that something had to give.

Roberto found a second job at Grady Hospital as a day-shift custodian, but with the substantially ridiculous daycare fee for Numa, on top of diapers and so forth, Roberto's additional paycheck was spent before he could cash it.

Then the twins were born. At that point, Numa was in the 1st grade—an innocently happy child who welcomed her newborn sisters home with open arms. But it wasn't long before Numa began to notice the strain of having the twins in the house—less food, less clothes, less toys, less attention. She began to hate the two little moochers who were eating them out of house and home, and wished for the will to throw them both from the upstairs window. That will never came about, and Numa didn't voice her grievance; she kept it bottled inside—something that she no longer does.

Then one bitter morning, just as the sun rose and the nightly fog dissipated, Calisa unconsciously entered room 246 instead of the charted check-out room, 245, whereupon noticing a man who was seated in the recliner, Calisa immediately apologized in Spanish before turning around to leave, but something told her to stop. Taking another look at the man, Calisa narrowed her eyes. His face was hidden behind a veil of dreadlocks, and if it weren't for the bloody white towel in his lap, she would've assumed that he was sound asleep.

Calisa spoke in Spanish. The man didn't stir. She eased closer—there was a backpack at his feet, beige in color and specked with blood.

The overhead light flickered, as most of them did whenever a dryer in the basement was turned on. Nonetheless, Calisa looked up at the light in a startled manner. Everything about this situation raised a red flag.

Calisa kicked at his shoe to awake him. "Hey?" she said, receiving no reaction.

She carefully brushed his dreadlocks aside with her hand and met his cold, dead stare. Calisa had seen many vacant souls in Puerto Rico, but that glossy, motionless glare was still very unsettling. A shiver clambered up her spine and she took a cautionary step backward. An instinct.

Reaching to open his coat, she paused to take a look over her shoulder—the door was open and anyone could've walked by and noticed her, so she quickly flapped the lapels of the peacoat open and saw that the man had suffered a gut shot. But how was it that no one heard the gunshot? Or was he possibly stabbed?

Calisa scanned the room. There was no sign of struggle. Her eyes settled on the backpack—something told her to take it and run, and that was exactly what she did.

The backpack contained two kilos of heroin and $6,000 in cash. Calisa immediately turned the bag over to Roberto, whose eyes stretched to the width of quarter pieces upon laying his peepers on the white gold.

"Our prayers have been answered," Roberto said tearfully.

The dead man was identified as one of four men who were involved in a deadly robbery in West Atlanta. The acknowledgment or whereabouts of a backpack was never in question.

Years had past and life was grand. Numa was gracefully progressing in one of Atlanta's most prestigious schools, and the twins never knew another night of hunger or cold beds. A nice house in Piedmont, fine automobiles, and fashionable clothes—the American dream that Roberto and Calisa wanted so badly had come true. Then a long-time customer of theirs was caught up in a sting in South Atlanta, in which the ATF and D.E.A. agents flipped him like a coin.

Numa witnessed the feds take everything from her—pinning her parents down to the floor with three consecutive life sentences apiece. Numa and the twins were placed in foster care—a system that allowed them to fall in between the cracks and eventually get separated altogether. Numa gathered the will and courage to escape, and that was when she actually felt and seen the heartlessness of the streets.

But now here she was, a madame with a stable full of ho's and a safe full of money. Her story was one for the books, and one day she'll ink a deal and tell it to the world.

Numa's phone chimed. After taking a sip of wine, she tapped on the screen of her phone to unlock it and saw that she had a text message from an unfamiliar number with an attachment.

(404) 881-2715: Amir's bitch ass is taken care of. No more worries, sis'.

A grin crept onto Numa's face. She opened the attachment. It was an image of Amir—a mugshot. He was being detained at the Fulton County Jail on first-degree murder charges—no bail granted as of yet.

Numa looked back to the city and took a deep breath of relief. She was nearly to the point of taking a leap of joy. Amir has caused her and her clients a great deal of grief and money—his removal has been on the table for quite some time.

The news of Amir's arrest made Numa's pussy wet. Turning away from the glass, she allowed her gown to fall from her body.

"Tutankha," Numa called the name of her South African escort.

Tutankha hurried across the floor. His long black dick swung between his legs.

"Yes, Madame?" he said.

"Tutankha," Numa said, reaching to stroke his manhood, "fuck me in my ass."

"Gladly, Madame," he answered.

"Then nut in my mouth."

"Only if you promise to swallow," he added.

With a mischievous grin, Numa bit down on her lip. "I promise."

Tutankha grabbed her strongly by her arm, whirled her around to the glass, and plunged his fingers inside her fat, wet pussy.

"But first I take care of her," Tutankha said, kneeling to eat her rosebud from the back.

Numa closed her eyes. “And you better not waste a drop, mothafucka,” she said, then moaned pleasurably. “Eat all that pussy.”

Chapter 32

Unita Williams was the owner of *WPK-Style Atlanta*, located on Upper Alabama Street. WPK was a butter-yellow triplex with oval-shaped windows and outdoor furniture. Unita converted the previously family-owned law firm into three businesses of her liking—a highly fashionable clothing store with oils and accessories, a salon/barber shop, and a popular radio station on the top floor that she hosted, called WPK, which were the initials of her deceased father, Wendall Pernell Keener.

Unita and her two sisters, Precious and KeKe, were currently on the air, nearing the close of their midday segment, REAL SPIT, which consisted of controversial topics and chart-topping hits of Hip Hop and R&B.

“Me, personally, I don’t get it,” Unita said in that sweet-sounding voice of hers. “I mean, these men, our black kings, ladies, choose to be in the streets. That’s a choice, right?” Her luscious, soft lips slightly brushed against the microphone. “Then they cry from their prison cell about not being able to see their kids or the feeling of being forgotten. Let’s—”

KeKe cut her off. “Which isn’t fair. Everyone makes mistakes, and—”

“Mistakes are a given, but these selective men who are slaves to the street life continuously make the same,” Unita stretched the word, *‘same’*, “mistake over and over again. How stupid are you to place your hand on a hot stove, twice!” Her voice rose with conviction. “Or more. A person who takes to a life of crime doesn't care about anyone but their damn selves. Period, boo."

"That's not true, Unita," Precious said defensively. "Now, granted that I don't condone such a life, I do know for a fact that a lotta people from the quote-unquote 'hood' put money back into their community, and—"

"Are you drunk?" Unita said sarcastically.

Precious made a face and said, "Be for real. I'm just saying that—"

"Cut the bull, alright? They're the reason that their communities are so damn jacked up in the first place. That so-called money that they put back into the neighborhood can't revive that little eight-year-old girl who died from a stray bullet, or that teenage boy who feels he needs the protection of a gang."

"No, but—"

"There are no buts, Precious!" Unita shouted, slamming her fist onto the table. "That money doesn't educate the youth."

"No, but it feeds a lotta hungry mouths."

"Educate them, and they'll learn a trade to feed themselves."

This shut Precious up.

Unita continued. "When white folks grab a sheet of paper to write down the words, 'Beating The Odds,' it should be spelled, 'B.L.A.C.K.' Period, boo."

"Where'd you learn that one?" KeKe wanted to know.

"Where I've learned it is unimportant. The fact that you now have it is everything, sis'," Unita responded sharply, then added, "But let's not deter from what Money Mike said in his letter—that black men are being taken from their children and blah, blah, blah, blah, blah, blah. Hey, Money Mike, news flash, asshole. You took yourself away from your children by willingly making the choice to sell Fentanyl, buddy."

KeKe shook her head. She disagreed with her sister, as always. "Whoa, now hold on a sec'. These men were born into poverty. Areas that lack proficient opportunities and education. How can they teach something that they've never been taught?"

Unita rolled her eyes. "Please," she scoffed. "With the same drive that they have to learn all of the wrong things, they can really turn things around for the better and become a productive black man in society, instead of a statistical slave to the judicial system like Money Mike and others who have written the station."

KeKe and Precious both shook their heads. Unita was a fave on the network, but damn, did people hate her—the truth hurt.

Precious sighed, then spoke into her microphone. "Well, that concludes today's show of REAL SPIT. Money Mike, keep your head up, and—"

Unita interrupted. "What she means is keep your head up out of your ass and into some books, pal. Become someone your children can be proud of, and stop letting these colonizers put you in chains."

Unita received a text message with an attachment. She didn't recognize the number. She opened the message just as KeKe was introducing a new song by Ella Mai.

(404) 881-2715: *Amir's bitch ass is taken care of. No more worries, sis'.*

Unita wrinkled a brow, and her heart rate quickened. Opening the attachment, she saw that it was an image of Amir—a mugshot. He was being detained at the Fulton County Jail on first-degree murder charges.

Unita quickly exited the room. She needed some fresh air—immediately. *What have they done?* Their fingerprints were all over that damn house. *How could CoCo be so fucking stupid?*

Unita was an independent woman who utilized her intelligence and boldness in a man's world, but there was one man who successfully broke through her barrier of protection and took possession of her heart—Amir Lathan, a dog-ass nigga from Bankhead.

Unita was raised in an area called Dixie Hills, which was not very far from the Bluff, in some apartments known as Shirley Place—a westside girl with a westside attitude. Growing up in Atlanta was an experience, an urban baptism of African American culture that had awarded her with richness and unwavering insight about the greatness of her people.

Unita was nothing like most girls back then, who only cared about popularity and making out with boys at Cascade. Unita's father, who was originally from Baltimore, Maryland, was an esteemed member of the Black Guerrilla Family (B.G.F.), and he made it his parental duty to raise her in the likeness of himself. So, while other girls were in school learning about how great white people were, Unita was at home with her father, learning about how devious those so-called "Greats" really were. As girls began to emerge into the stage of applying makeup on their faces and weave extensions in their hair, Unita's father taught her the importance and beauty of remaining natural—showing her what such products as perms and foundation truly did to black people's hair and skin in the long run.

Unita's father was a hardworking man, and after ten years of working as a forklift driver at the Coca-Cola plant on North Avenue, he quit to pursue his dream of opening his own restaurant. *We've worked for these crackers long enough, Unita. Always settle for having your own,* he once told her.

Unita used to catch the MARTA bus to 32nd and Bouldercrest on the eastside to help her father with the dinner crowd. It wasn't a very big restaurant, but her father's hometown recipes mixed with a little African flare filled the place to capacity every night. It was here that Unita learned the value of hard work and independence. She met people who were from all walks of life and normally grasped something new from every last one of them.

The restaurant was named Raven's Cove, stemming from her father's favorite football team, the Baltimore Ravens, but shortly after the grand opening, the locals began to call it Da' Cove.

Da' Cove was not upscale, nor was it located in the best of neighborhoods. Zone 3 was the biggest zone in Atlanta, but due to her father's limited price range, such localities with desirable scenery were not an option—5 Points, Castleberry Hill, Piedmont, even Ellenwood were not financially eligible for Unita's father, whose life savings did not amount to much in those days.

The staff mostly consisted of ex-cons who her father felt deserved a second chance at life, and with the help of their employees, Unita and her father would pass out free holiday meals and back-to-school supplies in Mountain Park and Sun Valley apartments off Bouldercrest—drug- and crime-infested areas with very little hope and assistance. Along with these gifts, they would also pass out literature by Noble Drew Ali and Marcus Garvey—words of affirmation and knowledge to abolish the indoctrination of Willie Lynch and historical white devils alike. A change was needed.

After several years of dedication, Raven's Cove finally began to turn a profit, and just when Unita's father was beginning to consider an additional location, tragedy struck. It was a bitterly cold night in January, and Atlanta was locked within a misty drizzle. It was minutes before closing. Unita was out back dumping the last bit of garbage in a bin when a gunshot caused her to stiffen.

"No!" screamed a woman.

Unita ran for the door. Her pulse was pounding as dreadful thoughts charged through her mind.

"Pernell?" Someone shouted her father's name.

Rushing into the dining room—there he lay, in the arms of Jameeka Clark—dead. Clutched in his hand was the shirt pocket of one of the masked robbers who he fought in defense of his employees.

"Dad?" Unita said, her voice shaky, skin suddenly itchy. "Daddy?" She fell to her knees and took hold of his hand. "Daddy?"

"They killed him," Jameeka said weakly. "Fuckin' crackheads shot 'em, Unita."

That was the rumor around Atlanta for several weeks—that two crackheads stormed into Raven's Cove and killed Pernell Keener—but the DNA, a skin particle that the medical examiner recovered from underneath Pernell's fingernails, proved otherwise. The crime was actually committed by two men who worked at Raven's Cove—violent offenders who were down on their luck before Pernell Keener took them in from out of the cold.

This horrible incident changed Unita for the worse—criminals sickened her. They were scum and cancerous to the communities. They could not be trusted, nor helped, and she made it a point to avoid their kind at all costs.

Unita was forced to move into her mother's house on Springside Run in Decatur. Unita and her mother, Trish, had never gotten along. Trish was lazy and commonly needed assistance to keep her, Precious, and KeKe afloat. Trish's alcoholism and outlandish behavior were what prompted Pernell to file for custody of Unita, in which Trish willingly signed over her rights.

After Pernell's death, Unita slid into a depressive state of mind, but with the help of her half-sister and her high school counselor, Mr. Jones, she gradually reappeared from the darkness.

Minutes after exiting *WPK-Style Atlanta*, Unita made her way past the Fountain of Rings at Centennial Olympic Park. She took deep breaths to calm her anxiety. She should have never set foot inside Amir and Alexandria's house last night.

The fountain, which blasted jets of water into the air, was teeming with children who were eager to shed the discomfort of the summer heat. A few men slung Unita a sultry eye. She was naturally fine—dark-skinned, petite with a bubble butt that jiggled whenever she walked. Her long dreadlocks were swept over to the left side of her head, resembling curly black rope that accentuated her round face and forest green eyes.

Up ahead, Unita saw a throng of runners pass by. Today was the Peachtree Road Race. Every 4th of July, some 55,000 runners braved the blistering heat to run 6.2 miles along Peachtree Street, past Lenox Square Mall, the glass tower of Buckhead, and the Woodruff Arts Center. Unita was currently feeling the need to do the same—run—but far, far, far away. No sooner than when she received the text message, Unita called Tink, who had friends in high places. Tink relayed the details to her of Amir's arrest. He killed Alexandria—or did they do it?

Unita took a seat on a bench and read the text message again. How had she fallen for such a man as Amir? Her father warned her of men like him, but it was fair to say that he deceived her. Amir Lathan was true to no bitch, but Alexandria didn't deserve to die—she was just as much a victim as any of them were.

Unita's phone rang. It was Numa calling. She answered on the third ring, saying, "Bitch, what the fuck happened?"

Chapter 33

Buckhead, one of Atlanta's wealthiest neighborhoods, was the last place Tink ever imagined her sister living. Eboni and Frank's house was nothing short of spectacular—an impressive glass structure with magnificent curves.

The temperature was seasonably warm for October—a graceful evening. After twelve long winters in Buffalo, New York, Tink was no longer accustomed to the mild winter tide of Georgia, but the small gathering in her honor was pleasant.

Eboni and Frank's backyard was a beautiful botanical garden that surrounded a heart-shaped swimming pool and hearth. The vascular plants shimmered in the silver light of the full moon, placing Tink in the mind of a luscious getaway—similar to St. Lucia, where she and her husband spent their 8-day honeymoon in 2013. Happier times.

The children were playing joyfully, running freely throughout the yard. Tink was eyeing her son curiously. Tonight was his very first time meeting all of his cousins, so he was in a rare form—a bundle of laughter and energy. Marquise was her world, her first and only child. His happiness means everything to her.

Tink inhaled the sweet smell of the apple-scented wood chips that drifted from the grill. Frank, who was wearing his well-renowned apron, "*I'm white, but like my lady well done*," was singing along with the music while seasoning a rack of lamb chops. Tink's siblings had informed her that Frank was a fantastic cook, and after arriving in Atlanta on an afternoon flight and being shuffled throughout the city by her mother, Tink was famished; or at least at the moment, she felt like she could eat a horse.

Seated near the fire of the hearth with her brother and two sisters, Tink took a sip of her pink champagne and savored the fuzzy explosion of bubbles. Laurent-Perrier Cuvée Rosé. She liked it, but she was quite certain that a bottle was well out of her price range. After twelve years of living off of a Navy salary, which was not very much, Tink had become somewhat of a penny-pincher.

Eboni looked at her Patek Philippe—7:15 p.m. "Momma should've been back by now," she said.

Tink's brother, the one who she has always been closer to, spoke. "The only thang momma have ever rushed was us," Seneca chuckled, revealing gold slugs in his mouth. "Rushed us out of her damn house."

With a sour expression, Monay, who has a lisp, mimicked their mother's high-pitched voice. "At seventeen and a half, you're getting the hell outta my house."

Tink laughed. "Oh my God. I hated when she said that shit," she said.

"She said it a lot," Eboni said.

Seneca, still flashing a bridge of gold, stretched his sandy brown eyes as wide as possible to emphasize his words. "A whole damn lot. I used to ask myself, '*Who the hell is she waiting to move in this muhfucka?*'"

Monay shot him a sideways glance, then rolled her eyes and said, "Nigga, you know who. If Drucker hadn't died, his black ass would've been housing shit up in that muhfucka right now."

"Dranking a big-ass cup of Kool-Aid and shit," Eboni added with a cackle. "That fuck nigga was always plotting on momma's cookie."

Tink's mouth fell open; she couldn't believe her ears. "What? Drucker?" she said. "The man with all of them keloids on his face?"

Monay snapped her fingers. “Yep. Muhfucka was dog-ass ugly, but word had it that the nigga had a kickstand for a dick.”

“Shid. Ol’ lady Kay called it a baby’s arm holding an apple,” Eboni said. “Would’ve bust momma’s lil’ ass up with that mothafucka.”

Seneca covered his ears. “Too much,” he said in a robotic voice. “Head. ’Bout. to. Ex. Plode.”

The sisters all laughed.

Then Tink waved her hand dismissively. “Bullshit,” she said, “Momma would’ve never touched that creep.”

“Tink, your ass was so caught up in DeAndre that you couldn’t see straight back then,” Eboni stated.

“All cock-eyed and shit ’bout that nigga,” Monay added.

“I often questioned if you even knew your own damn name when he was around, let alone aware of what the fuck was going on in Techwood.”

Tink had to agree with her sisters' colorful point of view. DeAndre was her high school sweetheart. A boy that persuaded her to flee Atlanta to enlist in the Navy when they were 18 years old . . . young, dumb, and full of cum. That was 24 years ago, and although her and DeAndre had broken up during their first tour, Tink never returned to Atlanta—not even to visit. So it was a celebration indeed.

Tink brushed a strand of her long black hair from out of her face, then looked at her son, reflecting to the time when her and DeAndre spoke of starting a family—which never happened. Men were low-down dirty dogs, mass manipulators who act as though they have a license to trample all over a woman’s heart, but this was the last time that she allowed some man to treat her like a doormat—she might very well just kill the next bastard who trespasses on her emotions.

Tink looked at her ring finger. Without the presence of her wedding band, it appeared out of place—as if it didn’t belong to her.

As Eboni and the others continued to converse about old man Drucker, Tink averted her eyes to the stars. A huge part of her missed New York, missed her husband and their perfect little brownstone apartment on Tanner Street that was only a block away from her favorite carry-out restaurant—best sesame chicken platter, ever.

"Tink?"

Tink looked at Eboni, and it was almost as if she was staring at herself in a mirror. Her and her siblings all shared various similarities, such as hazel brown eyes, mocha-colored skin, and dimples.

"You a'ight?" Eboni asked her, noticing her distant glare. "Come back to earth."

Tink forced a small grin. Eboni only knew one role—big sister. One who thought that she was their damn parent at times—even more so after their father was murdered.

"Yeah," Tink lied, "I'm good."

Marquise ran for his mother, shouting, "Mommy! Mommy!"

"Marquise, slow down before you fall," Tink told him.

Marquise, all but ten years old, was full of vigor and carbonated sweetener—soda pop, which Tink rarely allowed him to drink, but tonight was an exception and he was taking advantage of her leniency.

"Momma, uncle Frank said we can have some cake," Marquise said.

Tink looked at Frank questionably—he averted his smirk like a devious child.

"Uh, well, sweety, how about you wait for dessert," Tink said, "and get a little meat in that tummy first, kiddo." She tickled him, and he burst into a series of uncontrollable giggles.

Seneca, Monay, and Eboni all smiled warmly, because outside of the random video chats and holiday cards, it had been 24 years since they had seen Tink in the flesh, so to witness her motherly side was heart-touching.

Tink was with their father the day that he was stabbed to death in Bowen Homes. The unfortunate incident hardened her heart and it was the real reason that she fled Atlanta—DeAndre had only planted the notion of leaving, because she was already in search of an escape, mentally or physically, and the Navy provided her both. Tink spewed her pain onto terrorism in the Middle East. The strife and intricate missions of a Navy SEAL were a productive outlet that simmered her inner rage.

"Marquise, come on, they're winning!" Saniya, Monay's daughter, said.

Marquise darted off. Tink watched him. He looked so much like his father—it made her sick.

Seneca sighed. "One day Imma settle on down, y'all. Make a few jits of my own," he said.

By the term "jits," he was speaking of *children.*

Monay, who was taking a gulp of her red wine, nearly choked. Seneca was the biggest man-whore that any of them had ever known.

"Shid. As many ho's you be fucking around this bitch, I won't be surprised if—"

Seneca cut Eboni off. "Condoms. Yeah, it's a real thang, shawty."

"So is AIDS. Which you—"

"Nope. We ain't do that. Yo' boy Grade A, shawty."

"Fucking Grade E bitches," Monay said with a stank expression. "Sack-chasing ho's looking for rent money."

Seneca smiled. "Where would the world be without 'em?" he said, more so a statement.

They all laughed.

Seneca was a street nigga, the only one who followed in their father's shoes. Tink totally disagreed with his lifestyle, but that was a particular conversation that always fell upon deaf ears—he was in the mix far too deep for reasoning.

Frank reclaimed his seat next to Eboni, saying to everyone, "Food will be done in a few minutes." Then he looked at Tink. "So," he smiled, "Eboni said you're a cop."

"Detective," Tink felt the need to say, "but yeah."

Frank made a face that said, *Impressive.* Then he said, "Buffalo's a pretty rough city. 'Bout like Atlanta."

Tink agreed. "Yep. Whole lotta bad people out there."

Seneca and Monay looked at one another knowingly. As in "bad people," they knew that Tink was referring to Marion Wells—the man who murdered their father.

Eboni spoke, changing the subject entirely, but Tink kept her eyes on Frank. There was something oddly off about the man. A SEAL's survival rate is based upon being able to quickly identify shifty-looking individuals like Frank, who were most likely ragheads with bombs concealed underneath their garments. What was Frank hiding?

There's no way this man is a contractor, Tink told herself. *That's a quarter-million-dollar timepiece he's wearing. He doesn't even own a truck, for Christ's sake.* Tink looked toward the house—infrared cameras were positioned from every possible angle. Eboni had done exceptionally well for herself and her children, but at what cost? How did she end up with a white man and a glass castle?

Tink, who was around 5'10", stood up from her seat to excuse herself to the restroom.

"Want me to show you the way?" Eboni asked her.

"No, I can find it."

A minute later, Tink entered a bathroom of mass proportion, and with an effortlessly sexy walk, she made her way to the toilet, heels clicking against the marble floor. Unfastening the button of her skinny jeans, Tink pushed her panties and pants down past her thick thighs and took a seat.

The bathroom had vibrant green walls with unique patterns. Then there was the 13" camera monitor that was mounted above a frameless mirror. *Hmm?* Buckhead was one of the safest areas in the city. Criminals normally thought twice about embarking on the northside with unlawful intentions—so why so much surveillance?

Tink and her siblings were raised in the hood—Techwood, on the westside of the A', near the infamously vicious Bluff, so they were not strangers to volatile areas and could differentiate the likes of Buckhead and West Atlanta. Was Frank bent on protection as a whole, or was he keeping a watchful eye on something else entirely?

Tink reached for a pack of wet wipes, but a fluster of movement snagged her peripheral—prompting her to look at the monitor.

"Marquise!" she screamed.

Without another thought, Tink hopped up from the toilet and darted for the door, but forgetting to pull her panties and jeans up to her waist, she fell headlong across the floor. A burst of six rounds echoed loudly—*tat-tat-tat-tat-tat-tat!* "No!" Tink cried while scrambling to her feet.

Another six-round burst sounded . . .

. . . The ringing of Tink's phone snapped her out of her recollection of that horrible night. It's been six months since she buried her son, and her grief had only worsened.

Wiping tears from her eyes, Tink sat up from the sofa to retrieve her phone that was lying on the coffee table. It was Numa calling.

"Hello," she answered with a sniffle. Almost immediately, she added Unita to the call, and Numa heard the click of the call merging.

"Tink, what happened? Why you change the plan?" Unita heard Numa ask.

"I ain't change shit. Must've—"

"Somebody did," Unita interrupted, her voice sharp.

Tink felt a chill run down her spine. She knew this was about to escalate.

"Why'd you kill her?" Numa said.

Defenselessly, Tink responded, "I didn't fucking kill her!" she responded, panic creeping into her voice.

Then they all said simultaneously, "One of you bitches did it!"

Chapter 34

Two of APD's finest stared across the table at Amir Lathan. His ass was in a sling, and they both knew it, but a confession was always the goal for a detective.

Amir was a total wreck, at a complete loss—tapping his foot, fidgeting with his dreadlocks while still struggling to remember the details of last night.

Detective Kitson sized the murderer up. No tattoos or markings of any kind. No gold teeth or piercings whatsoever. Respectfully groomed and fit with no prior criminal history—this man did not meet the criteria of a senseless killer, but most of them never do.

Detective Harrelson also gathered an opinion of the killer. Tall, handsome, and strong—most likely known for pushing his weight around, even with her, up until the point of stabbing her in her damn neck.

"So, what you got for us, slick?" Kitson asked Amir.

Amir looked across the table at the beefy Black detective. He was an intelligent man who was normally in control of his emotions, but this was different—he literally did not know what the hell was going on. He did not kill Alexandria.

"I didn't do this. Alexandria was my heart," Amir said, a sadness deeply laced throughout his tone.

Harrelson, who Amir felt was in need of a tan, scoffed. "Bullshit. There's over fifteen domestic calls from your residence," he stated.

Amir shrugged. "So what, we fought. Doesn't mean I didn't love her."

"You don't beat on people you love, pal."

Amir's features tightened.

"Had she ever gotten the nerve to press charges, none of this may have happened," Kitson added.

Amir sucked his teeth irritably and snapped, "What the fuck do you know, nigga, huh? You—"

Kitson slammed his fist on the table. "I know you'll never see the light of day, motherfucker," he leaned across the table, "that's what I know."

With a menacing snarl, Amir shouted, "I didn't fucking kill her!"

"Then who did?"

"I don't know."

Harrelson grinned. "There he go," he said, clapping his hands. "Now that's the uncontrollable beast I was waiting to see."

With a look of disappointment, Amir lowered his head as if to shun away from the camera. The situation was getting the best of him.

Leaning back in his chair, Kitson averted his attention to the two-way mirror and said, "Play the recording."

The static crackle of speakers filled the room. Then, the recording that'll haunt Amir's thoughts for the rest of his life came forth.

"Nine-one-one," said a woman's voice. "What's your emergency?"

"Help, he's gonna kill me," was Alexandria's voice—trembly, whispery, but definitely her. "He has a knif—"

Next came the sound of someone kicking or pounding a door, possibly. Amir wasn't for certain what he heard.

Alexandria yelped frighteningly. "Amir, I'm sorry! I only slept with him once!" she shouted tearfully.

The sound of splintering wood followed. Alexandria screamed, then glass shattered and the sound of scuffling took over.

"Ma'am? Ma'am?" said the 9-1-1 operator.

"Stop, please!" Alexandria yelled, a painful cry that hurt Amir's heart to hear.

Then the call dropped.

Amir was completely stoked. He couldn't believe what the fuck he just heard, because to his knowledge, Alexandria had never cheated on him before. Confusion racked his brain. Why can't he remember anything?

"She stepped out on you, and you killed her for it," Kitson said.

"Bullshit."

"Guess another man named Amir did it, then?" Harrelson said sarcastically.

"Better off dead. Those are your words, aren't they?" Kitson wanted to know.

Amir thought about the words that were written on his bedroom wall in blood. He would've never done such a thing—he was a hood nigga, not some sadistic cult member. *Someone had done an incredible job of framing him for murder, forcing Alexandria to make a bogus 9-1-1 call, and all,* Amir told himself. *One of them bitter ass bitches did this. Or . . . them Augusta niggas.*

"I don't have nothing else to say to ya'll," Amir told them. "Take me to my cell."

The two detectives stared at him for an extended minute. He wasn't an easy nut to crack, but he was obviously emotional, so maybe just a little more push would be enough to shove him clean over the edge.

"Amir, listen. We can—"

Amir cut Harrelson off. "I'm done fucking talking."

With a heavy sigh, Kitson yelled for a deputy. "Take 'em."

"Say hello to the rest of your life, asshole," Harrelson said as the deputy was escorting Amir out of the room.

"It ain't over yet," Amir countered.

While walking down a corridor, Amir looked down at his wrists—chained like a slave. Beaten and outsmarted by a calculated killer who was most likely feeling quite smitten with their self at the moment. Amir was an official street nigga who was normally the most intelligent man in the room—so how was he outwitted? And how in the hell is he going to rise from the ruins of this predicament unscathed?

Amir was from West Atlanta—Ashby Street, just up from Harris Homes that was known for heroin and common gunplay, but other hoods such as Etheridge Court and Bowen Homes were his stomping grounds as well. Money, cars, clothes, and ho's was his thing, and Amir Lathan had many things, but none of it mattered if he couldn't wiggle out of this bind.

Amir was just like any other kid growing up. He had big dreams of becoming the best lawyer in Atlanta, or a rich doctor, or an airplane pilot—so many dreams, but none of them came true. He was instead pushed to the streets at the tender age of fourteen years old . . .

. . . Darren smacked Keisha in her face and she fell against the wall—knocking a lamp to the floor.

"Darren, stop!" she cried.

Drunk and wobbly, Darren pointed an unsteady finger at her and slurred, "Sass me again, bitch, and see what I do, hear?"

With blood between the cracks of her teeth, Keisha shouted, "I didn't—"

"Shut up!"

"Momma?" Amir said sleepily while descending the steps.

Darren looked over his shoulder at Amir with a hooded gaze. "Nigga, get back upstairs right now before I —"

"No," Amir said in a steely tone of voice. "Leave my momma alone."

"Amir, get to your room," Keisha told him.

Amir was fed up with his stepfather's abuse. Darren was strung out on crack; hours after giving Keisha the monthly bill money, he always returned home drunk and high, demanding that she give him his money back, and beat her if she refused to do so.

Darren turned around and rushed Amir with a number of sluggish blows. Amir staggered to the floor. The taste of blood was immediate—he underestimated the bastard.

Darren kicked Amir in his face, then he grabbed him by the collar of his shirt and pulled him toward the front door. Amir was dazed and seeing doubles.

"Darren, no!" Keisha cried.

Pinky and Mellow were standing at the top of the staircase—crying their eyes out as their father tossed their brother onto the porch like a disobedient dog.

"Amir!" Pinky yelled. "Don't leave me!"

Darren slammed the door with his foot, then warned Keisha, "Go out that door and your ass gone stay out there with 'em."

"That's my son, Darren."

"You heard what I said, dammit. Now try me."

Spitting a glob of blood on the porch, Amir took hold of the banister and pulled himself up to his feet. The wintry December air caused him to shiver.

He waited for the door to open, for his mother to tell him to get his ass in the house and go to his bedroom . . . but all was quiet. Then someone parted the living room curtains—it was his mother.

"Get the fuck away from that window!" he heard his stepfather yell, and she quickly shut the curtains.

The white glow of the porch light shimmered in his watery eyes as he struggled to stable himself.

"Now give me my damn money, woman. I won't tell ya' again."

Amir descended the steps of the porch; his socks did nothing to ward off the chill of the cold pavement—he felt every jagged groove of the walkway. Could it have been more fractured than his hopeless-ass life?

Amir stopped to look up at his sisters' bedroom window—broken up and teary-eyed, they waved goodbye. This crushed his heart. He didn't want to leave Pinky and Mellow. Who was going to make them breakfast every morning? Walk them to their bus stop? Protect them?

Amir headed down the street. He didn't have anywhere to go, but with every step he took, his soul darkened. How could his mother just leave him out in the cold like this? He was her flesh and blood, her only son.

His aunt, Kat, and uncle, Vell, both lived in Jonesboro South—completely across town, for which he had no cash for transportation nor a call.

Amir rubbed his bare arms, then he cupped his hands around his mouth and blew, and blew, and blew.

Entering an abandoned house, Amir stepped cautiously around drug paraphernalia—syringes especially. The place reeked of piss and shit—a shithole. Guided by streams of moonlight, Amir entered the living room where a mangy sofa and damaged coffee tables were positioned in the middle of the floor. Kicking a few empty beer cans aside, Amir reached to the floor for a dusty blanket, but he paused upon hearing something outside of one of the glassless windows.

"Bitch, where the fuck you think you're going, ho?"

"T.L., I'm sorry, that's all I—"

"Don't be sorry, be careful, ho. Careful 'bout coming short on my goddamn skrilla, bitch."

Amir eased to the window and saw Tough Love roughing up one of his girls—Janeen—pretty, but highly underage.

Tough Love grabbed Janeen by her throat and forced her against the side of the house. Instinctively, Amir took a cautious step backward and stepped onto something sharp. A yelp escaped his throat and he quickly slapped a hand over his mouth and looked down at his foot.

"Who in there?" Tough Love yelled.

Tough Love was bad news, and Amir didn't want to be on the other side of the man's pistol for eavesdropping on his conversation, so he ran for the door.

"Come here, goddammit," Tough Love said upon grabbing Amir by his arm as he exited the house . . .

. . . "Hey, Gentry," squawked a voice through the deputy's radio.

"Gentry here," the deputy spoke into his device while veering a corner of the corridor with Amir.

"When they're done with Lathan, take him down to VR2; he has a visit."

"A visit?" Gentry said questionably. "But today isn't visitation day, Sarg."

"Just do it, a'ight?"

"Copy that. I'm en route now."

Amir arched a brow but remained quiet because Gentry knew just about as much as he did—nothing. Who has the authority to visit an inmate on unscheduled days? Lawyers? Feds? Who? Pinky? Mellow? Could a pair of ruthless Queens pens pull something like this off? Tough Love? Who?

Upon entering the visitation room, Amir's question was answered, but he could hardly believe his eyes. His breathing quickened, and an anger so immense clogged his vision that he began to see red blotches. Standing on the opposite side of the plexiglass was a ghost. *He killed this bitch.*

Gentry closed the door and stood guard in the corridor. Amir was paralyzed in thought, uncertain what to think or say. He had obviously fallen for a honey trap, but how?

She took a seat.

So did he.

They stared into one another's eyes. Tink was beautiful, but her bitterness shimmered throughout her eyes like the light that danced across her gold doorknocker earrings. She hated him. He loved her. *Shit happens and hearts get broke in the process, but that's life.* Tough Love used to always tell him when he was a boy, "A woman is one of the most dangerous creatures on the planet, Amir, so it's smart to break her spirit down to the smallest molecule, early!"

Tink reached for the telephone receiver. Amir did the same. No one immediately spoke. Pain—and so much of it.

"I killed you," Amir finally said.

She agreed. "Inside, yes."

Her short, clipped response irritated him, and he said angrily, "How the fuck are you alive, bitch?"

Tink's calm demeanor dissipated and she snapped, "You can't kill what's already dead, fuck nigga," her voice cracked, "you ripped my fucking heart out of my chest with this shit."

Amir's features tightened. "You killed Alexandria, didn't . . ."

Numa and Unita walked into view and Amir's words trailed off.

"Hell is about to rain down on your ass, nigga," Tink said, "and we got front row seats."

With a grit, Amir said, "Well, strap in for one helluva show, bitch. 'Cause if you think for one minute Imma lay down and wear this charge, you're stupid." He looked to Numa and Unita. "Fuck you ho's. My sisters'll handle you bitches."

Numa, Tink, and Unita smiled. They all knew something that he didn't.

To be continued

Lock Down Publications and Ca$h Presents Assisted Publishing Packages

Due to an increase in the price of services we have increased our prices. The prices below reflect the price increase as of 11/1/24.

BASIC PACKAGE **$699** Editing Cover Design Formatting	**UPGRADED PACKAGE** **$1000** Typing Editing Cover Design Formatting Upload eBooks to Amazon Upload Paperback to Amazon
ADVANCE PACKAGE **$1,400** Typing Editing (line editing/content) Cover Design Formatting Copyright Registration Proofreading Upload eBooks to Amazon Upload Paperback to Amazon	**LDP SUPREME PACKAGE** **$1,700** Typing Editing (line editing/content) Cover Design Formatting Copyright Registration Proofreading Set up Amazon Account Upload eBooks to Amazon Upload Paperback to Amazon Advertise on LDP's Amazon and Facebook Page

***

Other services available upon request.
Additional charges may apply

Lock Down Publications
P.O. Box 944
Stockbridge, GA 30281-9998
Phone: 470 303-9761
Email: lockdownpublications@gmail.com

Submission Guideline

Submit the first three chapters of your completed manuscript to ldpsubmissions@gmail.com. In the subject line add **Your Book's Title**. The manuscript must be in a Word Doc file and sent as an attachment. Document should be in Times New Roman, double spaced, and in size 12 font. Also, provide your synopsis and full contact information. If sending multiple submissions, they must each be in a separate email.

Have a story but no way to send it electronically? You can still submit to LDP/Ca$h Presents. Send in the first three chapters, written or typed, of your completed manuscript to:

LDP: Submissions Dept
P.O. Box 944
Stockbridge, GA 30281-9998

DO NOT send original manuscript. Must be a duplicate.
Provide your synopsis and a cover letter containing your full contact information.

Thanks for considering LDP and Ca$h Presents.

NEW RELEASES

BLOODLINE OF A SAVAGE 1-3
THESE VICIOUS STREETS 1-3
RELENTLESS GOON 1-3
SOULLESS GOON 1&2
BY PRINCE A. TAUHID

THE BUTTERFLY MAFIA 3
BY FUMIYA PAYNE

A THUG'S STREET PRINCESS 1&2
BY MEESHA

CITY OF SMOKE 1-3
BY MOLOTTI

GET IT IN SLUGS 1 &2
BY B. STALL

STANDING ON HER BUSINESS 1&2
BY DG SANTANA

STEPPERS 1,2&3
THE REAL BADDIES OF CHI-RAQ 1-3
BY KING RIO

THE LANE 1-3
BY KEN-KEN SPENCE

THUG OF SPADES 1&2
LOVE IN THE TRENCHES 1&2
CORNER BOYS 1&2
ONCE YOU GO GANGSTA
PROTÉGÉ OF A LEGEND 1- 3
BY COREY ROBINSON

TIL DEATH 3
BY ARYANNA

THE BIRTH OF A GANGSTER 4
BY DELMONT PLAYER

PRODUCT OF THE STREETS 1-3
BY DEMOND "MONEY" ANDERSON

MONEY HUNGRY DEMONS 1-2
BY TRANAY ADAMS

TRAP STARS
BY B. SHELLY

HUB CITY MENACE 1-4
BY J. WHITE

A THUGGISH PASSION 1&2
LAND OF DA HOOLIGANZ 1-4
KILLAZ ON STANDBY 1&2
FRESH OFF DA PORCH 1-3
SECURE DA BAG
AMBITIONS OF A SLIDER
FOR MY ENEMIES SAKE
SOULLESS GOON 1&2
FO'EVA ROLLIN 1-4
BY ASSA RAYMOND BAKER

THE LEVEL UP 1&2
BY LUXURY KING

HUNGRY FOR MONEY 1&2
SLIMBOS

QUEEN OF NAPTOWN 1&2
THA TAKEOVER 1-3
BY KEITH CHANDLER

DRILL CITY 1&2
BY ZAY'TOWVEN

LOVE ME OR LET ME GO
BY R. FACEY

SAVAGE DREAMZ
BY KING DAVID

MONEY AND DEAD HOMIES
BY DERRICK SUMMERS

WHITE BOYS
BY BANDEMIC

A THUGS STREET PRINCESS 3 Coming Soon
BY MEESHA

BETRAYAL OF A G 2
BY RAY VINCI

SAVAGE FAMILY EMPIRE 1&2
SOULLESS GOON 1&2
THE DIRTY SIDE OF MONEY 1,2&3
BY PRINCE

BY THE TRUCKLOAD 1-4 COMING SOON
T SOULLESS GOON 1&2
IPPIN' THE SCALES 1-4
BAD BITCHES WIT GUNZ 1-3
PROBLEM SOLVED 1-3
THE GIRLRILLA AND HER N*GGA
THE SINGLE LADIES
BY CHRISTOPHER "DIESEL" HORNEZES

AVAILABLE NOW

RESTRAINING ORDER 1 & 2
BY CA$H & COFFEE

LOVE KNOWS NO BOUNDARIES 1-3
BY COFFEE

RAISED AS A GOON I, II, III & IV
BRED BY THE SLUMS I, II, III
BLAST FOR ME I & II
ROTTEN TO THE CORE I II III
A BRONX TALE I, II, III
DUFFLE BAG CARTEL I II III IV V VI
HEARTLESS GOON I II III IV V
A SAVAGE DOPEBOY I II
DRUG LORDS I II III
CUTTHROAT MAFIA I II
KING OF THE TRENCHES
BY GHOST

LAY IT DOWN I & II
LAST OF A DYING BREED I II
BLOOD STAINS OF A SHOTTA I & II III
BY JAMAICA

LOYAL TO THE GAME I II III
LIFE OF SIN I, II III
BY TJ & JELISSA

IF LOVING HIM IS WRONG…I & II
LOVE ME EVEN WHEN IT HURTS I II III
BY JELISSA

PUSH IT TO THE LIMIT
BY BRE' HAYES

WHITE BOYS 2 | BANDEMIC

BLOODY COMMAS I & II
SKI MASK CARTEL I, II & III
KING OF NEW YORK I II, III IV V
RISE TO POWER I II III
COKE KINGS I II III IV V
BORN HEARTLESS I II III IV
KING OF THE TRAP I II
BY T.J. EDWARDS

WHEN THE STREETS CLAP BACK I & II III
THE HEART OF A SAVAGE I II III IV
MONEY MAFIA I II
LOYAL TO THE SOIL I II III
BY JIBRIL WILLIAMS

A DISTINGUISHED THUG STOLE MY HEART I II & III
LOVE SHOULDN'T HURT I II III IV
RENEGADE BOYS 1-4
PAID IN KARMA 1-3
SAVAGE STORMS 1-3
AN UNFORESEEN LOVE 1-3
BABY, I'M WINTERTIME COLD 1-3
A THUG'S STREET PRINCESS 1,2&3
EMBRACING THE LOVE OF A BOSS
BY MEESHA

A GANGSTER'S CODE 1-3
A GANGSTER'S SYN 1-3
THE SAVAGE LIFE 1-3
CHAINED TO THE STREETS 1-3
BLOOD ON THE MONEY 1-3
A GANGSTA'S PAIN 1-3
BEAUTIFUL LIES AND UGLY TRUTHS
CHURCH IN THESE STREETS
BY J-BLUNT

CUM FOR ME 1-8
AN LDP EROTICA COLLABORATION

BLOOD OF A BOSS 1-5
SHADOWS OF THE GAME
TRAP BASTARD
BY ASKARI

THE STREETS BLEED MURDER 1-3
THE HEART OF A GANGSTA 1-3
BY JERRY JACKSON

WHEN A GOOD GIRL GOES BAD
BY ADRIENNE

THE COST OF LOYALTY 1-3
BY KWELI

BRIDE OF A HUSTLA 1-3
THE FETTI GIRLS 1-3
CORRUPTED BY A GANGSTA 1-4
BLINDED BY HIS LOVE
THE PRICE YOU PAY FOR LOVE 1-3
DOPE GIRL MAGIC 1-3
BY DESTINY SKAI

A KINGPIN'S AMBITION
A KINGPIN'S AMBITION II
I MURDER FOR THE DOUGH
BY AMBITIOUS

TRUE SAVAGE 1-7
DOPE BOY MAGIC 1-3
MIDNIGHT CARTEL 1-3
CITY OF KINGZ 1&2
NIGHTMARE ON SILENT AVE
THE PLUG OF LIL MEXICO 1&2
CLASSIC CITY
BY CHRIS GREEN

GANGSTA CITY
BY TEDDY DUKE

BACK IN BLOOD
SEX, MURDER AND GOD 1&2
COUNTDOWN OF A KILLA 1&2
GUNS DOWN, BOTTOMS UP 1&2
BY LO-LIFE

A GANGSTER'S REVENGE 1-4
THE BOSS MAN'S DAUGHTERS 1-5
A SAVAGE LOVE 1&2
BAE BELONGS TO ME 1&2
A HUSTLER'S DECEIT 1-3
WHAT BAD BITCHES DO 1-3
SOUL OF A MONSTER 1-3
KILL ZONE
A DOPE BOY'S QUEEN 1-3
TIL DEATH 1-3
IMMA DIE BOUT MINE 1-6
DYING FOR LIKES 1&2
KILLA CREW 1&2
BY ARYANNA

A DOPEBOY'S PRAYER
BY EDDIE "WOLF" LEE

THE KING CARTEL 1-3
BY FRANK GRESHAM

THESE NIGGAS AIN'T LOYAL 1-3
BY NIKKI TEE

GANGSTA SHYT 1-3
BY CATO

THE ULTIMATE BETRAYAL
BY PHOENIX

BOSS'N UP 1-3
BY ROYAL NICOLE

I LOVE YOU TO DEATH
BY DESTINY J

I RIDE FOR MY HITTA
I STILL RIDE FOR MY HITTA
BY MISTY HOLT

LOVE & CHASIN' PAPER
BY QAY CROCKETT

TO DIE IN VAIN
SINS OF A HUSTLA
BY ASAD

BROOKLYN HUSTLAZ
BY BOOGSY MORINA

A DRUG KING AND HIS DIAMOND 1-3
A DOPEMAN'S RICHES
HER MAN, MINE'S TOO 1&2
CASH MONEY HO'S
THE WIFEY I USED TO BE 1&2
PRETTY GIRLS DO NASTY THINGS
BY NICOLE GOOSBY

LIPSTICK KILLAH 1-3
CRIME OF PASSION 1-3
FRIEND OR FOE 1-3
BY MIMI

TRAPHOUSE KING 1-3
KINGPIN KILLAZ 1-3
STREET KINGS 1&2
PAID IN BLOOD 1&2
CARTEL KILLAZ 1-3
DOPE GODS 1&2
BY HOOD RICH

WHITE BOYS 2 | BANDEMIC

BROOKLYN ON LOCK 1 & 2
BY SONOVIA

THE STREETS ARE CALLING
BY DUQUIE WILSON

STEADY MOBBN' 1-3
THE STREETS STAINED MY SOUL 1-3
BY MARCELLUS ALLEN

WHO SHOT YA 1-3
SON OF A DOPE FIEND 1-4
HEAVEN GOT A GHETTO 1&2
SKI MASK MONEY 1&2
BY RENTA

GORILLAZ IN THE BAY 1-4
TEARS OF A GANGSTA 1/&2
3X KRAZY 1&2
STRAIGHT BEAST MODE 1&2
BY DE'KARI

SLAUGHTER GANG 1-3
RUTHLESS HEART 1-3
BY WILLIE SLAUGHTER

GOD BLESS THE TRAPPERS 1-3
THESE SCANDALOUS STREETS 1-3
FEAR MY GANGSTA 1-5
THESE STREETS DON'T LOVE NOBODY 1-2
BURY ME A G 1-5
A GANGSTA'S EMPIRE 1-4
THE DOPEMAN'S BODYGAURD 1&2
THE REALEST KILLAZ 1-3
THE LAST OF THE OGS 1-3
BY TRANAY ADAMS

MARRIED TO A BOSS 1-3
BY DESTINY SKAI & CHRIS GREEN

TRIGGADALE 1-3
MURDA WAS THE CASE 1-3
BY ELIJAH R. FREEMAN

KINGZ OF THE GAME 1-7
CRIME BOSS 1-4
BY PLAYA RAY

FUK SHYT
BY BLAKK DIAMOND

DON'T F#CK WITH MY HEART 1&2
BY LINNEA

ADDICTED TO THE DRAMA 1-3
IN THE ARM OF HIS BOSS
BY JAMILA

YAYO 1-4
A SHOOTER'S AMBITION 1&2
BRED IN THE GAME
BY S. ALLEN

TRAP GOD 1-3
RICH $AVAGE 1-3
MONEY IN THE GRAVE 1-3
CARTEL MONEY 1&2
BY MARTELL TROUBLESOME BOLDEN

FOREVER GANGSTA 1&2
GLOCKS ON SATIN SHEETS 1&2
BY ADRIAN DULAN

TOE TAGZ 1-4
LEVELS TO THIS SHYT 1&2
IT'S JUST ME AND YOU
BY AH'MILLION

LOYALTY AIN'T PROMISED 1&2
BY KEITH WILLIAMS

KINGPIN DREAMS 1-3
RAN OFF ON DA PLUG
BY PAPER BOI RARI

THE STREETS MADE ME 1-3
BY LARRY D. WRIGHT

CONFESSIONS OF A GANGSTA 1-4
CONFESSIONS OF A JACKBOY 1-3
CONFESSIONS OF A HITMAN
CONFESSIONS OF A DOPE BOY
BY NICHOLAS LOCK

I'M NOTHING WITHOUT HIS LOVE
SINS OF A THUG
TO THE THUG I LOVED BEFORE
A GANGSTA SAVED XMAS
IN A HUSTLER I TRUST
BY MONET DRAGUN

QUIET MONEY 1-3
THUG LIFE 1-3
EXTENDED CLIP 1&2
A GANGSTA'S PARADISE
BY TRAI'QUAN

CAUGHT UP IN THE LIFE 1-3
THE STREETS NEVER LET GO 1-3
BY ROBERT BAPTISTE

NEW TO THE GAME 1-3
MONEY, MURDER & MEMORIES 1-3
BY MALIK D. RICE

CREAM 2-3
THE STREETS WILL TALK
BY YOLANDA MOORE

THE STREETS WILL NEVER CLOSE 1-3
BY K'AJJI

LIFE OF A SAVAGE 1-4
A GANGSTA'S QUR'AN 1-4
MURDA SEASON 1-3
GANGLAND CARTEL 1-3
CHI'RAQ GANGSTAS 1-4
KILLERS ON ELM STREET 1-3
JACK BOYZ N DA BRONX 1-3
A DOPEBOY'S DREAM 1-3
JACK BOYS VS DOPE BOYS 1-3
COKE GIRLZ
COKE BOYS
SOSA GANG 1&2
BRONX SAVAGES
BODYMORE KINGPINS
BLOOD OF A GOON
BY ROMELL TUKES

CONCRETE KILLA 1-3
VICIOUS LOYALTY 1-3
BLOODY MONEY BAGS
BY KINGPEN

THE ULTIMATE SACRIFICE 1-6
KHADIFI
IF YOU CROSS ME ONCE 1-3
ANGEL 1-4
IN THE BLINK OF AN EYE
BY ANTHONY FIELDS

THE LIFE OF A HOOD STAR
BY CA$H & RASHIA WILSON

WHITE BOYS 2 | BANDEMIC

NIGHTMARES OF A HUSTLA 1-3
BLOOD AND GAMES 1&2
BY KING DREAM

HARD AND RUTHLESS 1&2
MOB TOWN 251
THE BILLIONAIRE BENTLEYS 1-3
REAL G'S MOVE IN SILENCE
BY VON DIESEL

MOB TIES 1-7
SOUL OF A HUSTLER, HEART OF A KILLER 1-3
GORILLAZ IN THE TRENCHES
OOPS CRY TOO 1-3
THE DAUGHTER OF A CARTEL BOSS 1&2
BY SAYNOMORE

BODYMORE MURDERLAND 1-3
THE BIRTH OF A GANGSTER 1-4
BY DELMONT PLAYER

FOR THE LOVE OF A BOSS 1&2
BY C. D. BLUE

KILLA KOUNTY 1-5
TENDER 1&2
BY KHUFU

MOBBED UP 1-4
THE BRICK MAN 1-5
THE COCAINE PRINCESS 1-10
STEPPERS 1-3
SUPER GREMLIN 1-5
A GANGSTA'S SON
THE CONNECT'S SECRET
BY KING RIO

MONEY GAME 1&2
BY SMOOVE DOLLA

WHITE BOYS 2 | BANDEMIC

A GANGSTA'S KARMA 1-5
BY FLAME

KING OF THE TRENCHES 1-3
By GHOST & TRANAY ADAMS

QUEEN OF THE ZOO 1&2
BY BLACK MIGO

GRIMEY WAYS 1-3
BETRAYAL OF A G
BY RAY VINCI

XMAS WITH AN ATL SHOOTER
BY CA$H & DESTINY SKAI

KING KILLA 1&2
PAPER, ROCK, SNAKES
BY VINCENT "VITTO" HOLLOWAY

BETRAYAL OF A THUG 1&2
BY FRE$H

COUNTDOWN OF A KILLA 1&2
SEX, MURDER AND GOD 1&2
GUNS DOWN, BOTTOMS UP 1&2
BY LO-LIFE

FOR THE LOVE OF BLOOD 1-4
BY JAMEL MITCHELL

HOOD CONSIGLIERE 1-3
NO TIME FOR ERROR 1&2
REAL
BY KEESE

THE PLUG'S RUTHLESS DAUGHTER 1,2&3
REDEMPTION IN THE STREETS
BY TONY DANIELS

WHITE BOYS 2 | BANDEMIC

BORN IN THE GRAVE 1-3
CRIME PAYS 1-3
BY SELF MADE TAY

MOAN IN MY MOUTH
BY XTASY

TORN BETWEEN A GANGSTER AND A GENTLEMAN
BY J-BLUNT

LOYALTY IS EVERYTHING 1-3
CITY OF SMOKE 1-3
BY MOLOTTI

HERE TODAY GONE TOMORROW 1&2
BY FLY ROCK

WOMEN LIE MEN LIE 1-4
FIFTY SHADES OF SNOW 1-3
STACK BEFORE YOU SPLURGE
GIRLS FALL LIKE DOMINOES
NAÏVE TO THE STREETS
BY ROY MILLIGAN

PILLOW PRINCESS
BY S. HAWKINS

THE BUTTERFLY MAFIA 1-3
SALUTE MY SAVAGERY 1&2
BY FUMIYA PAYNE

THE LANE 1&2
BY KEN-KEN SPENCE

THE PUSSY TRAP 1-5
BY NENE CAPRI

DIRTY DNA
BY BLAQUE

SANCTIFIED AND HORNY
BY XTASY

BOOKS BY LDP'S CEO, CA$H

TRUST IN NO MAN
TRUST IN NO MAN 2
TRUST IN NO MAN 3
BONDED BY BLOOD
SHORTY GOT A THUG
THUGS CRY
THUGS CRY 2
THUGS CRY 3
TRUST NO BITCH
TRUST NO BITCH 2
TRUST NO BITCH 3
TIL MY CASKET DROPS
RESTRAINING ORDER
RESTRAINING ORDER 2
IN LOVE WITH A CONVICT
LIFE OF A HOOD STAR
XMAS WITH AN ATL SHOOTER

www.ingramcontent.com/pod-product-compliance
Lightning Source LLC
LaVergne TN
LVHW020716110826
845149LV00012B/2291